KATHARINE O'NEILL

Sergeant Silver

Happy Birthday!

Love Katharine
K O'Neill

First edition

This book was professionally typeset on Reedsy.
Find out more at reedsy.com

Contents

Chapter One

E mily had planned to make the most of a free morning. That wasn't something she got to do every day. After having breakfast and taking a leisurely shower, she had settled down to read. Another one of her favorite things Emily had been unable to enjoy recently. Things were just far too busy right now.

Like surviving.

But the headache that had been building since the day before was too much. It pressed down hard over her temples and over her eyes. Her stomach was churning as well, stress tying her up in knots.

Maybe if she just closed her eyes for a moment, see if some brief meditation helped…

Next thing she knew, Emily was jerking herself awake as a loud shrill alarm threatened to burst her eardrums, filling the entire apartment with shrieks that any toddler would be proud of. It took her a moment to realize that it was her cell phone's alarm. Telling her to leave the house.

Telling her that she was going to be late for work.

Shit. Not what I need right now.

Getting ready wasn't a problem. That could be dealt with easily. But getting to work was going to be a nightmare. Her apartment was on the outskirts of Union, and the traffic just before the lunch hour was always bad. But nothing would compare to this.

It was the Super Bowl, and the Carolina Panthers were taking part in it for the first time in a long time. So those who were going to watch on big screens in the city or heading over to watch with friends and families would turn the place into gridlock.

Who knew that South Carolina would be proud of a North Carolina team?"

Emily could feel the panic growing as she tried to negotiate shortcuts to work, only to find that everyone else was going the same way. Mike was going to be furious when she finally turned out. He hated tardiness. And Emily was only a week out of her probationary period.

Emily understood why he hated lateness. But she didn't want to be on the receiving end of it.

It was forty-five minutes after the start of her shift that Emily managed to pull into a space of the employees around the back of Mike's Barbecue and Grill. With any luck, he wouldn't be in. On a Sunday, he was watching his daughter play softball in her Sunday league, leaving new supervisor Callie in charge until mid-afternoon. She could let Emily get away with being late, especially on Super Bowl Sunday.

Hopefully.

Emily scurried through the back door and into the locker room. Opening up her locker, wincing as she scraped her arm along the metal, Emily put her bag inside and tugged off her t-shirt. It was early February, but it was warm enough inside that working in a t-shirt wouldn't be too much of a problem.

Picking out her work t-shirt, a dark blue polo top with a collar, Emily turned as she began to put it on. And then she froze.

Mike Wilson was in the doorway, staring at her with his arms folded.

Emily's mouth went dry as she stared at the six-one lean body of her boss. Wearing jeans and a blue shirt with the sleeves rolled up, the man emanated an intensity that had Emily's legs going weak. A persistent throbbing would start between her legs whenever Mike was nearby. It was distracting.

Ever since she had been introduced to Mike three months ago, Emily couldn't stop herself from giving him the onceover. And another. And another.

Damn. Who knew fifty could look so good?

"You're late."

Emily could not get enough of that voice. Even after living in South Carolina for the last fifteen years, Mike's accent was still firmly in the middle

2

of England. It was beautiful to listen to. Better than the usual southern drawl that was common in the state.

Then Emily remembered where she was. She was at her place of work, showing her bra to Mike. Feeling her face getting warm, Emily quickly turned her back on him and pulled on her t-shirt.

"Sorry, Mike." She mumbled. "The traffic was crap."

"Really?"

"Really."

Emily turned back, adjusting the collar on her shirt, only to catch Mike looking at her backside. *Was he checking me out?* Emily had been aware of Mike watching her, but he was her boss. And a soldier. They were naturally suspicious.

But not like this. Like she was a woman and not an employee.

Mike's eyes flicked back up and they locked gazes. Had his eyes changed color or were they always that shade? Emily bit her lip and put her hands behind her back. Her fingers were itching, yet again, to reach out and touch him. To see if that chest of his looked as solid as she imagined.

Stop it. This is dangerous. You need to get your mind focused.

For a moment, Mike looked like he was about to say something. Then his expression hardened and he straightened up.

"I'll let this go for now, Molly." He said gruffly. "Two more strikes, though, and I'll have to let you go. I can't have anyone slacking here."

"Yes, Sir."

Emily bit back a grimace. Molly. God, she hated that name. Why couldn't she have been allowed to pick it out? But everything had been selected for her. Her name, her location, even her job. It was like she wasn't trusted to do it herself.

Emily had wanted to have something that wouldn't have her forgetting who she was. Her middle name of Jessica would have sufficed. But now she was stuck with Molly.

Everything about her had to be simple, mundane. Nothing to draw attention to herself, and that included being tardy with a job Emily hated.

Mike left the room, and it was only then that Emily felt like she could breathe again. God, the man was a presence that she was more than aware of. And she wasn't the only one. Mike could walk through the restaurant and every woman from the customers to the waitresses would watch him go. It was like people queued up to get his attention.

Emily had never been one of those people who fell over herself to get anyone's approval - that sort of thing was frowned upon where she had come from - but she found herself wanting to do something so her boss would notice her, just for a moment.

Preferably when they weren't the only ones in the locker room and Emily was half-dressed.

But you certainly won't say no if it happens again, will you?

Damn right I won't.

God, she needed to get a job elsewhere. She was meant to be in hiding, not fantasizing about the ex-army restaurateur. It didn't matter how handsome he was, she shouldn't be doing it.

Emily locked her things away and hurried through the kitchen, entering the restaurant behind the bar. The lunch crowd wasn't as high as it normally was - a surprise, considering the Super Bowl was on - but it was beginning to pick up.

Callie was behind the bar, collecting an order from one of the waitresses. She gave Emily a grin, her tight black curls bouncing about her face.

"Hey, you. I was beginning to wonder where you were. Mike was beginning to doubt my excuses about you."

"Considering how inventive your excuses are, I'm not surprised." Emily retrieved an apron from under the bar and tied it around her waist. "I got caught in the Super Bowl traffic. Mike wasn't happy, but he let me off, thank God."

"Wait, what?" Callie stared at her. "Mike actually took a reason for being late and didn't give you a warning?"

"No, there was no warning." Emily felt like she was being stared at as if she was an exotic fish in a tank. "Why are you looking at me like that?"

"I'll tell you in a minute." Callie gestured at a couple who had just entered the bar. "Let me deal with them first."

"As she headed off to greet the newcomers, Emily made her way to the restaurant side of the building, reaching the waiter's station. The smell of the grill and the thick barbecue sauce that the chefs prepared on the day could be smelled from across the building. Emily took a moment to take a deep breath and inhale this through her nostrils.

This was the only part of the job she did like. Other than a handsome boss. Emily loved steak - she loved meat in general - and she adored barbecue. It did mean working for hours with her stomach growling, but the staff got free meals on their break. Emily was happy with free food, and she couldn't get enough of the barbecue wings.

Even with that plus, Emily's old job was far easier than dealing with the general public.

"Mike let you come in and work without a warning?"

Emily turned. Callie was walking towards her, looking at Emily with barely contained confusion. Emily frowned.

"What's wrong with that?"

"What's wrong is that he doesn't give anyone a second chance on anything, and that includes tardiness. You make one mistake here and you're on a warning. Second mistake, and you're out."

"Everyone makes mistakes. Isn't that usual in businesses?"

"Not on small things. Mike expects people to work and obey like he's still in the army." Callie folded her arms. "He has fired people on the spot when they come in five minutes late. You're the first person, from my knowledge, that he's ever been lenient towards about timekeeping."

Emily rolled her eyes.

"Come off it, Callie. It's Super Bowl weekend. He knows that the traffic is going to be shit. Any other decent boss would understand and let it slide."

"Well, all I can say is I've never seen him do that before. Not even when his ex's little sister worked here back when you joined." Callie whistled. "And boy, did she push it."

Emily could still remember that. Dawn was a spoiled little brat who thought she was entitled to anything because her sister was dating the owner. She had been fired before the end of her third shift after coming to work half an hour late, saying that she had been washing her hair and making it look nice. After her first warning about getting the orders wrong and putting the blame onto Emily, that was her out the door.

Emily had never seen such gall from anyone. If Dawn had been in the army, she would have been drop-kicked out of there so fast she wouldn't have the chance to bounce. And Emily would love to do the kicking.

"What do you think it means for me?" She asked. "That Mike's finally going soft?"

Callie smirked.

"I think he's got a thing for you."

Emily blinked. Mike had a thing for her? Surely, that wasn't possible.

"What makes you say he has a thing for me?"

"You're not stupid, Molly. You have eyes. He has to fancy you for him to let you off with a warning when he would have done worse. And from the way he's been looking at you since you came here…" Callie pressed a hand to her chest with a wistful sigh. "Well, let's just say if I had a man looking at me like that, I would be on him like white on rice."

For a moment, Emily's mind went blank. She was used to men flirting with her. That she could handle. But this? It wasn't possible, was it? Wasn't she too young for Mike? Surely, he would look for someone nearer his own age.

That didn't make Emily feel any better.

"He doesn't look at me in the way that you're suggesting."

"Why not? You're hot, he's hot, and you're both single."

"I'm going to pretend I didn't hear you call me hot."

Callie laughed.

"I don't mince my words. And you are."

"Hmm." Emily shook her head. "As you said, we're both single. Mike only very recently. Why would he be thinking about someone else when he's just come out of a relationship where he was put through the wringer?"

Callie rolled her eyes.

"Don't be naive, Molly. Take a look next time you see him. I'm not wrong about what I've seen."

"I think you are."

"Bet you twenty dollars that he does fancy you."

Emily burst out laughing.

"You're betting on that?"

Callie shrugged.

"What can I say? It keeps things interesting around here."

She had a point. Waitressing kept them busy, but Emily was bored up to the eyeballs with it. She could walk away from it, but then her superiors would be furious. Emily had been given an option, and if she didn't take it, there was going to be a big fallout. She didn't want to go through that.

And also she wasn't one to pass on a bet.

"Done. Besides," she picked up a spare notepad and pen from the waiter's station, "I can't afford a relationship right now. Too much baggage makes things messy."

Callie giggled.

"Who said it had to be a committed relationship? You could have a one-night fling?"

"Callie, that's not what I do. And certainly not with my boss."

Certainly not with Mike Wilson. That would be particularly messy. Emily didn't think she could keep sex and her emotions separate. Mike elicited something really strong inside her, and that scared her. It was far too intense.

"That's a pity." Callie was still giggling as she walked away. "Because I think Mike would be up for it if you asked."

Emily didn't think so, even if the thought of approaching Mike for it made her feel hot under the collar. She was an employee, Mike was her boss. Both of them were from the same lifestyle that made crossing that line out of bounds.

Besides, having Mike calling her Molly while he was fucking her was going to be more than a mood killer.

#

Mike couldn't stop himself from staring at Molly as she went about the tables. She was like a beacon to him. Not very tall but her vibrant red hair, long and thick, tied back in a simple plait made her stand out. Up close, he could see her cornflower-blue eyes, and they always seemed to be sparkling with something. They drew him in. And that body of hers…Mike had only ever seen body frames that compact and muscular in the army. Lithe and firm in all the right places.

Especially that ass, hugged nicely in her jeans. Every time she leaned over, Mike's eyes were drawn to Molly's backside. He itched to go up to her and just touch her. See if that ass was as firm as it looked.

But he shouldn't. He shouldn't even be looking at her like that. Mike had a very firm rule about dating employees. Sleeping with one of his waitresses was not a good idea.

Especially with a waitress young enough to be his daughter.

Mike hadn't intended to walk into the locker room, planning to wait until Molly was coming out. He had been about to reprimand her for being late, that she was to finish off her shift and not come back; he couldn't break his own rules for her.

Then he had seen Molly taking off her shirt, revealing an underwired bra that hugged her pert, firm breasts. It left little to the imagination. It had taken Mike a lot of self-control not to press her against the locker and have a taste.

He needed to get his mind out of the gutter.

"Evening, Mike."

Mike jumped. A gruff, big man in his late thirties sporting a thick black beard had slid onto a stool in front of him. Mike reached for a pint glass.

"Same as usual, Will?"

"Please." Will Carruthers tapped the counter with his hands. "I'm thirsty."

Will was only a recent regular, but he had been coming into the bar every day since moving to Union a month ago. He always stuck to the bar, though, spending hours talking to whoever was working. The ladies seemed quite charmed with him.

"You're always thirsty, bud." Mike pushed a full glass across the counter and took Will's money. "I'm surprised you don't have beer in your veins with the amount you drink."

Will laughed.

8

"I probably do." He raised his glass in a toast. "But I'm not going to slit my wrists to find out."

He took a large gulp with a satisfied sigh. Mike watched him as he started cleaning glasses. Will was a big man, hefty but it was a weight he carried well. He was light on his feet. Mike could spot another squaddie a mile off, but Will was always silent on it.

Mike could understand. He could only imagine the horrors that kept the man's mouth shut. It kept his shut on a good day, never mind a bad day.

"How's the new girl coming along, then?"

"Hmm?" Mike looked up. "New girl?"

"The redhead in the restaurant." Will nodded at the mirror behind Mike. "The one with the pert bum."

That was another thing about Will. He never looked into the restaurant. He always kept his back to that side of the room, using only the mirror above the bar to look. Mike had never figured out why he did that.

He looked over at Molly, who was standing at a table where a family of six were sitting, laughing at something the mother said. There were smiles all around the table. Molly had the ability to do that to everyone she came across. The patrons loved her. She was bright and friendly, and could put everyone at ease. Even the rowdier ones. The woman was like a magnet.

Mike was certainly drawn to her.

"Molly? She's doing fine. The woman is a harder worker than I am."

"I see." Will waggled his eyebrows." Just the way you like them, eh?"

"I don't fraternize with my employees, Will. And they don't fraternize with the customers during shifts, either, so don't get any ideas."

Will grunted.

"Pity. I was thinking of asking her for a drink. Not here, of course," He tapped the bar with a broad finger, "Or you'd be glaring at us all the time."

Mike grunted, resisting the urge to snap something back. Why did the thought of Molly being on a date with Will form a knot in his stomach? Then again, he couldn't see Molly agreeing to a date. Will certainly did not seem her type.

Mike knew he was very lucky to have found Molly. A former army buddy had introduced them, saying that Molly was looking to start afresh and was looking for a job. Mike had been a little reluctant to take her on as Molly had no waitressing experience, but he was glad he had agreed. Molly had been invaluable. Her ability to learn fast had astounded him.

He just wished that his friend hadn't given him a gorgeous woman who distracted him just by smiling.

"What is her story?"

"Sorry?"

"Molly." Will raised his eyebrows. "What's her story?"

"Why do you want to know?"

"Because I'm a nosey bugger."

"You haven't asked about the rest of my staff." Mike folded his arms. "Why should I tell you about Molly?"

"You're her boss. And I'm curious."

Mike shook his head.

"You want to know anything about Molly, you ask her. It's not my place to say."

It was then that Mike heard raised voices. He looked over and saw Molly at another table, this one a booth crowded with college jocks. One had stood up and was trying to grab her backside, attempting to pull her into the booth. Molly slapped his hands away and stood her ground even as the jock towered over her.

Mike's protective instinct then went into overdrive. He put his things aside.

"Excuse me a moment, Will. I think one of my staff needs some help."

"Lucky them." Will grunted. "Wish I could get my hands on sweet little Molly."

Mike ignored this. He was too focused on the jock taking a swing at Molly.

Chapter Two

There were times when Emily hated being a waitress and drunk patrons who thought she was part of the menu was one of those times. The more they guzzled back, the more aggressive and hands-on they became. A lot of them eventually backed down once Molly gave them a slap on the hand and a glare.

But some, like the jock who had been touching her hip and backside whenever she went past, just didn't seem to be getting the message. Emily gritted her teeth and carried on serving them. She wanted to smash her tray over his head, but she was already on thin ice. She couldn't afford to be fired.

To say her superiors wouldn't be impressed would be an understatement. But there was only so much Emily could handle before her patience went down. And it had worn down a lot in the last month.

So when the jock openly grabbed her backside as she was placing the fifth round of drinks on his table, Emily calmly put the drinks down and then jammed the edge of the tray against his arm. The jock yelped and pulled back.

"What the hell?"

Emily sneered at him.

"Oh, I'm so sorry. I get a little jumpy when someone grabs me when I didn't consent."

"Aw, come on, sweetie." The jock sat forward and leered at her. "Can't you have a bit of fun?"

"I'm here to work, not to have fun."

"Fancy working on me, then?"

The young man looked over her body with open appreciation. Emily had a sudden urge to shower that look away. She slapped at his hands as he reached for her again.

"You couldn't handle me."

One of his buddies burst out laughing.

"She's a fiery one."

"Perfect." The jock stood and grabbed Emily's wrist, tugging her so she fell against his chest. "I like my girls to have a bit of fire."

He stank of alcohol and bad body odor. Emily gritted her teeth as his fingers dug into her skin.

Now she didn't care if she was fired. She wasn't about to take this, and they had been warned. She rammed her knee up into his crotch. The jock moaned and doubled over, his hand loosening on her wrist. Emily pulled away, spun the idiot around and twisted his arm up behind his back. Then she shoved him face-down onto his table. Drinks toppled over, alcohol all over the table, and there was the sound of breaking glass.

"Hey!"

The other college kids tried to get away before their drinks went all over them, jammed in the booth with their exit blocked. The jock in Emily's grip tried to get up, but Emily flattened him more onto the table, twisting his arm until he squealed.

"I told you that I wasn't part of the menu, sir." She hissed.

"You little bitch" He struggled, but he couldn't get up. "Let me go!"

"That's enough!"

Emily abruptly let go of the drunk and stepped back with her hands raised as Mike stormed across the room towards them. His eyes were blazing. The idiot straightened up with a grimace, flexing his arm, and squared up to Mike.

"She nearly broke my arm!" He bellowed, pointing at Emily. "I want her fired!"

Mike pushed Emily behind him and folded his arms with a scowl.

"And I saw you groping her. That's the fourth time you've done it that I've witnessed. What have I told you about getting hands-on with my staff when you were last in here?"

"She attacked us!"

Mike held up his hand and then signalled to one of the waitresses. She hurried to the bar and picked up the cell phone they kept behind the counter.

"You've got three seconds to get out of here before I call the police. And all of you are barred."

"On, come on!" One of the mates whined. "You're going to believe her?"

Emily growled, but Mike gave her a look that made her back down.

"Are you saying that I need to get my eyes checked, sir? Because I saw what happened. And we will have CCTV footage to back me up." He nodded at the cameras dotted around the room. "Now, get out of here before Simon starts dialling. Three, two..."

"Okay, fine." The idiot Emily had grappled with was the first to move, cradling his arm against his chest. "We're going. This place is a dump, anyway."

He pushed past Mike and purposefully bumped Emily's shoulder. His friends also glowered at Emily, but they kept their distance. It wasn't until they were walking out the door that Emily could feel her pulse slowing back to normal.

Then Mike turned to her, and her pulse rate picked up again. Why did he have to stand so close?

"Go to my office, Molly."

"I'm sorry..."

"Go."

Lowering her head, Emily hurried off to the staff only door and up to Mike's office. Once inside, Emily found herself pacing, unable to sit with her nerves going. She needed to save her job somehow, even if it meant going on her knees and begging. There was no excuse for violence.

What was Chambers going to say? He had told her to keep her head down. Do nothing that would draw attention to herself. Emily had asked how she was supposed to do that when she had red hair, to which Chambers had no answer. They had stopped arguing about Emily dying her hair to a more neutral, nondescript color. No way was Emily dying her hair. She was already being forced into hiding; she wasn't losing her hair as well.

Emily managed to get a speech ready in her head, but when Mike came into the room five minutes later, her mind went blank. Being alone with him had her insides feeling like she was caging butterflies. She gulped.

"I'm so sorry about that, Mike. I shouldn't have…"

"Slow down, Molly." Mike closed the door and approached her. "You're not in any trouble. I just thought you might want to take a moment before you went back out."

"What?" Emily's mouth fell open. "You're not going to fire me?"

"Why would I do that?"

"Because I attacked a customer."

"And I saw what they were doing. It's not the first time those cocky sods have molested my staff. You're just the first who fought back."

Then he took her hand, lifting her wrist to reveal the red marks where the college brat had grabbed her. His fingers felt like they were burning her skin. Emily had always prided herself on being in control, but that control disappeared with Mike. Very rapidly.

"How's your wrist?"

"Hmm?" Why did that accent have to send a shiver down her spine? "It's sore but I'll live. I've had worse."

"Worse?" Mike's eyes widened. "Someone's attacked you before?"

"I don't go looking for it." Heat was travelling up her arm from where Mike was holding her hand. She eased her hand away, rubbing her wrist. She was aware of her face getting warm. "I'm fine."

He was standing too close. And he didn't seem to be in any rush to move away. Emily moved back, leaning against his desk. She needed to; her legs were feeling like they were going to give way.

"Where did you learn to defend yourself like that?" Mike asked.

"Why do you want to know?"

"I'm curious." Mike folded his arms. "That college upstart is twice the size of you, yet you managed to practically bend him in half."

Emily absently rubbed at her wrist.

"My dad. He wanted me to take care of himself."

"I bet you were that girl who loved all the action movies."

"Horror movies, actually."

Mike raised an eyebrow.

"So, you're a girl who likes to be scared."

"Only when it's not happening to me."

Mike laughed.

"I don't think I'll ever understand you, Molly."

Molly. Emily was beginning to hate that name. And talking to Mike when they were alone was asking for trouble. Emily straightened up and carefully stepped around him, trying not to look him in the eye.

"I…I'd better get back to work. It's busy today and I…I need to go."

"Molly…"

She could feel Mike reaching for her, but Emily stepped out of reach. She tried not to run across the room, her hands fumbling for the door handle.

"Thanks for the breather, Mike, but I'm okay now. I'll get back to work."

Then she was yanking the door open and hurrying down the stairs. It had been years since Emily had felt like a high school girl with her first crush. And it was something she was still not used to.

#

Mike was glad when it was the end of the shift. It had been a very busy afternoon once custom picked up; football games brought in a lot of people celebrating their bets on the Super Bowl. His staff were clearly exhausted, but still managed to go around with big smiles.

Especially Molly. She was running around like someone had wound her key up too tight. There didn't seem to be an off-switch with her. Mike had to stop himself from staring at her as she worked. Every time she was on shift, he ended up floundering. There was no chance of keeping his eyes off Molly when she was in the restaurant.

Mike had spent years in the army controlling his emotions and keeping himself focused. It had been beneficial to him when starting up his business, and now his training had gone ever since Molly came into his life. The intensity of how affected he was shook him as well. Not even his ex-girlfriend did that to him.

15

Callie let the last customer out and closed the door. She walked back towards the kitchen with a wave at Mike.

"Night, Mike. You staying late?"

"I have to. I've got the books to do." Mike found his glasses and propped them up on his head. "I'll leave the keys in your mailbox when I leave. I have a feeling I'm going to be having a lie-in after all this."

"No problem." Callie gave him a salute. "Night, Sergeant."

She left the bar. Mike came out from behind the bar and sat at a table with a heavy sigh. He opened up the accounts book, wincing when he saw the date of the last time he had written in it. It didn't look any better when he put his glasses on. Molly had offered to put it into the computer for him to make things easier, but Mike preferred the paper trail; it wouldn't get lost in cyberspace.

Now he was beginning to wish he had accepted her offer.

Mike pushed this aside. He couldn't afford to think about Molly right now. His head needed to get into sorting these figures out or he was going to be here all night.

Mike growled when he heard the door opening. They had the closed sign up. Surely that meant not to come in? He turned around to snap at the late night guest, only to see the strawberry-blonde beauty coming towards him. Petite and slender, wearing a pale green skirt suit with her hair tied back in a tight bun, she looked every bit the professional. Even with the legs that seemed to go on for miles.

Mike groaned. He didn't want to see her and she knew that she wasn't welcome on his premises. He turned back to his books.

"Go away, Carol. Can't you see we're closed?"

"Can't I get a drink?" Carol asked. "You always got me a drink even after you'd called time."

"That was when we were dating. You're an ex now, and you'll be treated like everyone else." Mike pushed his glasses up his nose. "Get out. Now."

For someone who worked in the US attorney's office, Carol Grimshaw didn't use her brains when she was supposed to. Dumb and stubborn. Mike had been driven to distraction by the stubborn side of her. It grated on his nerves. He had called time on their relationship six weeks before, but Carol just wouldn't leave him alone. She kept coming to find him every other day, pleading with him to take her back.

Mike wasn't about to be cuckolded for a second time.

The chair across the table scraped along the tiles, and Mike glanced up to see Carol sitting down. She unbuttoned her jacket to reveal a simple white blouse, giving Mike a sad smile as she sat back.

"You're not answering my calls, Mike."

"I don't want to talk to you."

"You're going to need to talk to me sometime."

"No, I don't." Mike glared. "You betrayed me, Carol, and I kicked you out of my life. Simple."

Mike didn't want to remember when he came home to find his girlfriend in bed with a colleague of hers. They hadn't even tried to hide it, both of them laughing. Mike had kicked them both out. Everything had ended that night. Carol hadn't taken it well, still half-naked as she pleaded with him.

She had done it to herself and yet she expected them to go on as normal. Mike wasn't stupid. Carol would certainly not take any responsibility. She thought she just needed a pretty smile and flash her legs to get what she wanted. Not with him anymore.

"Please, Mike." Carol insisted. "Can't I apologize for what I did?"

"No." Mike shook his head. "I'm not a doormat, Carol. You can't walk all over me."

"It was one mistake."

"One mistake is enough." Mike lowered his pen with a scowl, slamming his glasses onto the table. "If you messed up, it's your problem, not mine. Take responsibility for your actions." He pointed at the door. "Now, get out of here before I call your boss about harassment. They're not going to like that."

Carol's jaw tightened, but she didn't move. Sighing heavily, Mike stood and came around the table. He grabbed Carol by the arm and hauled her to her feet.

"God, you're like an underdone piece of toast that keeps popping back up."

He began to drag her towards the door, snatching her jacket off the back of her chair. "When I end something,I really end it. No pieces to pick up or anything. Just…" He opened the door, pushing her out into the street. "Just get out of here."

"I still love you, Mike." Carol turned back to him, cupping his face in her hands. "I do."

"It's not mutual." Mike shook her off with a growl. "Now, out!"

Unceremoniously, he practically shoved her out the door before closing it with a bang. As a quick afterthought, Mike found his keys and locked the door. Carol banged on the glass, gesturing at him to let her in. Mike took out his cell phone and held it up to her before he started dialling.

That had Carol scurrying away. Mike sighed and dropped his cell back into his pocket. It was going to be a long night.

Chapter Three

Emily yawned and rolled her shoulders as she shrugged off her shirt. The muscles in her back and neck were knotted up to the point of painful.

"Thank God that's over."

"I know." Callie was changing three lockers down, putting on a black t-shirt. "I swear days when the football is on are the worst."

"And it's going to be even worse in a week or two." Emily made a face. "Valentine's Day."

"You don't like Valentine's Day?"

"Not really." Emily hung up her shirt and put on her t-shirt, tugging her hair out of the neck hole. "Too lovey-dovey for my liking. I've had too many bad things happen on Valentine's Day. That's enough to put me off."

It was Valentine's Day when things started that turned her life upside-down. The day which eventually culminated in Emily being stuck in Union pretending to be someone she wasn't. As far as she was concerned, Valentine's Day could go to hell.

The two women headed out into the parking lot. Mike was still inside, finishing off before he locked up. Even as she left, Emily felt like Mike was watching her. She could feel the hairs on the back of her neck standing up, a warm shiver curling around her spine. The man was too distracting for her own liking. Emily had been close to giving in and that was just after one month. How was she going to cope with a longer period of time?

She shivered as a cold wind rippled under her collar and down her back. In her haste earlier, she had forgotten to bring her jacket along. Goosebumps were tickling her arms. She wrapped her arms around her middle and hunched against the wind.

"Where's your coat, Molly?"

"Hmm? Oh." Emily had used false names before, but it still took some getting used to. "I left it behind. I forgot to bring it."

"In this weather?"

"I know. I'm an idiot."

Callie laughed.

"I won't argue with that." She fished out her keys and unlocked her car, giving Emily a wave. "Night."

"Night."

Then Emily saw Callie's eyes flicker to a point over Emily's shoulder. It was very brief, and then Callie was getting into the car. No further reaction.

Probably a trick of the light. Emily's paranoia was getting to her.

She walked over to her own car as Callie drove away, exhaustion beginning to finally set it. Waitressing was not a job she would have done willingly, and Emily could see why; it felt like it could mentally destroy you.

Emily was getting out her keys when she heard footsteps behind her. Instinct made Emily turn around, her hand going into her bag. She couldn't carry a gun on her, but she did have mace. The can was out and coming up before Emily saw who was walking towards her.

And it had her almost dropping the can in shock. Tall, muscular, broad with skin so dark it was almost ebony and his hair cut close to his head. Even in civilian clothes, it was clear that he was army. He slowed as Emily backed up, peering at her curiously.

"Emily? Is that you?"

Panicking, Emily looked around them. There was nobody there, but she still lowered her voice.

"Don't say that name out loud!" She hissed.

Darryl Houghton-Leathers moved closer. His eyes widened.

"My God. I thought I was seeing things."

"Yeah, well, maybe you should have." Emily put the mace away. Much as she wanted to use it on him, she was more concerned about getting away.

"What are you doing here, Darryl?"

"I just got stationed at Fort Jackson. I'm here to see some friends."

"I didn't know you have friends in Union."

"Well, I've got friends everywhere." Darryl frowned, lowering his hands. "What about you, Emily? What are you doing here? I didn't know you were nearby."

That was the point. Even if Emily wasn't in hiding, she wouldn't have told her former boyfriend where she was going. The man had sided with the wrong people, and Emily couldn't forgive that. Even if Darryl wanted to reconcile.

"You know I can't discuss anything, Darryl. Technically, I'm not supposed to be here."

"You..." That was when realization dawned. "You mean you're..."

"Yes." Emily pointed at him. "And if you let anyone know that you've seen me, you'll be putting me in danger."

"I would never do that to you! You know I wouldn't."

"And I would agree on that if you weren't so close to the man who tried to kill me." Emily snorted. "My superiors are still trying to figure out how he got into my house without breaking in."

Darryl's mouth fell open.

"You think I gave him a key?"

"What am I supposed to think?" Emily snapped. "I ended it with you the week before. Maybe it was revenge."

"Emily, no!" Darryl shook his head. "I still love you, you know that."

They had been together a long time. Darryl had dropped hints about getting married. Now that was gone after Emily discovered Darryl's link to her case. And she couldn't bring herself to feel anything for him anymore.

They were out in the open. Someone could hear them, and Emily was a non-moving target. She needed to get out of there.

"I don't trust anyone right now, Darryl. People are trying to kill me." Emily backed towards her car. "You must not say a word to anyone. If something happens to me, I'll know exactly who leaked my location."

Darryl's eyes narrowed.

"You're threatening me now, are you?"

"To keep myself alive, absolutely. And if you have to talk to me, my name is Molly. As far as anyone's concerned, Emily's dead."

"Okay." Darryl hesitated. "Can I see you again?"

God, the man was persistent. Emily had to give him that. Up until she had had to disappear, Darryl had texted her and called her, trying to get her to change her mind. Emily didn't want to think about how many times he had changed her mind on anything over the years.

"It's best that you just forget about me and go back to Fort Jackson." Emily fumbled for the door handle. "Bye, Darryl."

Jumping into the car, Emily slammed the door shut and put the central locking on. She could see Darryl still staring at her, but he didn't move. Emily turned on the engine, put her car into gear, and tore out of the parking lot.

#

All Mike wanted to do when he got home was go to his bed, bury himself under the duvet and refuse to come out again. Why did that woman have to keep coming back? Mike had made it perfectly clear that he would not tolerate any kind of cheating.

When they had first met, he had thought Carol was it. She was smart, beautiful and glamorous. But any love Mike had for her had died six weeks ago. He couldn't stay with someone who thought it was okay to cheat on him.

Mike pulled into the carport outside his house and got out, taking a deep breath as he squeezed past a small Ford Fiesta that was parked haphazardly in the space next to him. The lights were on inside, even at this late hour. His daughter was home, more than likely talking to one of her many friends.

Mike entered his house and heard Prudence's voice coming from the living room.

"He did? No! Then what happened?" Then she gasped. "Carly! Now I wish I hadn't asked." She giggled. "Serves you right for going out with him. Now you know why his nickname is The Octopus."

Mike entered the living room and saw his eighteen-year-old daughter sprawled out on the couch, her cell phone glued to her ear. Books and her laptop were spread out on the coffee table and the carpet. Studying appeared to have taken a back seat.

"Am I interrupting something?"

Prudence looked up and gave him a grin. Her dark hair was loose about her shoulders, her eyes sparkling.

"Sorry, Carly, I've got to go. My dad's come back. I won't say a word about this, I promise. Bye." She hung up, sitting up and swinging her legs off the couch. "Hey, Dad."

"Hey, you." Mike leaned over and kissed her head. "The Octopus? What kind of nickname is that?"

Prudence giggled.

"He's the quarterback at school. Carly had a date with him tonight."

"He has hands all over the place when he's playing?"

"Not just when he's playing football."

Mike rolled his eyes, dropping his backpack on the floor and kicking off his boots.

"I came in at the wrong moment. Sounds like you didn't get the juicy bits."

Prudence laughed.

"Dad! I swear you're more of a gossip than I am!"

"Well, if I live with a teenager, what do you expect?" Mike limped over to his chair and eased into it. It was after long days that his knee injury started complaining. "What are you doing up, anyway? You've got school tomorrow."

"I've got an exam tomorrow." Prudence gestured at her books. "I'm just doing some last-minute revision."

"And talking about The Octopus was revision?"

"A nice break. Besides," Prudence folded her arms with a smirk as she sat back, "At least I'm focused. I'm not letting someone get in the way."

"What's that supposed to mean?"

"Come on, Dad. You know exactly what I'm talking about."

"No, I don't, and I'm too tired to have a cryptic conversation."

Prudence laughed.

"I'm talking about that new waitress at your place. Molly Ferrel. Every time

I'm in there, I catch you looking at her. It's certainly not how an employer should look at someone who worked for them. I'm surprised you manage to work at all when you're following her around the room with your eyes."

Mike could feel his face getting warm.

"Don't be ridiculous, Prudence." He grumbled. "Just because I think Molly is attractive doesn't mean I'm going to do anything about it. You know my rules. And, in case you've forgotten, I've just got out of a relationship. I'm not ready to dive back into another one."

"From the way you've been behaving, I'd say you are." Prudence curled her legs up underneath her. In black yoga pants and a baggy green t-shirt, she looked very young and fresh-faced. "It would be nice to see you with someone who's not going to mess you around. From what I know of Molly, she certainly won't do that to you."

"Since when have I asked my daughter for advice?"

"Well, you haven't got anyone else to ask."

Mike sighed. Prudence was an adult now, and it had been just the two of them for the last ten years since Mike's wife Melissa had died. She had been the victim of a drunk-driver slamming into her car, and the sudden loss had left Mike in pieces. He had only just been discharged from the army due to his injuries, and now his wife was gone. If it hadn't been for Prudence, only eight years old at the time, Mike would have gone off the tracks a long time ago.

They didn't need anyone else in their life. Although Carol had been a big possibility over the last three years. And that hadn't come to fruition.

"I wouldn't object, Dad."

"Sorry?"

"If you started dating Molly. I like her." Prudence smiled. "She'd be good for you."

"I've already told you, Prudence. I don't date my employees."

"Rules are made to be broken."

"Not with me."

Rules had been drilled into his head in the army. They were there for a reason, and Mike's own imposed rules had never been broken. Even as tempting as Molly Ferrel was to him, Mike wasn't about to start now.

"You say that now," Prudence said, "but one day someone's going to snap her up and you're going to regret not asking her out."

"And I regret not going to bed as soon as I got in." Mike snorted. "I can't believe I'm listening to a teenager telling me how to get a woman to date me."

Prudence laughed.

"You don't have to listen to me, you know."

"Thank God for that." Mike yawned and eased himself to his feet. "It's getting late. I'm going to get something to eat and then go to bed. You'd better get some sleep as well."

"I've still got some revision to do." Prudence waved at her books. "I'm nearly done."

"You're not going to be able to drive in if you're too tired."

Prudence's eyes twinkled as she grinned slyly up at her father.

"That's because you're going to drive me in."

She was a pest. But Mike couldn't deny her even that. He groaned and threw up his hands.

"Fine. I'll drive you in."

"Thanks, Dad." Prudence beamed. "You're the best father."

Mike didn't answer that.

Chapter Four

Emily didn't see a car following her as she made her way back to her apartment. But that didn't stop her from taking a very long, circuitous route back in the hope of shaking any possible tail. After meeting Darryl – whether by accident or by Darryl's design, Emily didn't know – she was paranoid.

What if Marsden was after her now? Would Darryl have said something to him? If Marsden found her now, at least Emily knew who had spilled the beans. The two men were close. They had started at the academy together. A bond like theirs wouldn't be broken that easily.

Emily didn't want to hang around to find out.

She finally made it to her apartment, pulling into a spot a block away. Then she took the back streets, ducking and sprinting through the alleys, and entering the tradesmen's entrance. She took the elevator to her floor and ran along the hall, her hands fumbling with the keys in the lock. It felt like forever before Emily managed to get into her apartment, slamming the door behind her and leaning on it. Her heart was racing.

If anyone had managed to find her after that, they were a better tracker than Emily anticipated. As of now, she could feel relatively safe in the knowledge that she hadn't been followed.

If only she could relax.

Slumping to the floor in a heap, Emily found her cell phone. Chambers needed to know. He would be furious to find out someone had stuck a squaddie with a connection to Emily so close by. Whoever had done that would be in serious trouble.

Chambers picked up on the fifth ring before it went to voicemail. His voice was thick with sleep.

"Chambers."

"It's me."

"I didn't realize you'd become my personal alarm clock, O'Rourke."

"You what?" Emily checked the time. "It's twelve-thirty here, and you're three hours behind me. You can't be in bed right now."

"Who said I was sleeping?"

Oh. Emily cringed. That was not an image she wanted.

"Sorry, Sir. But this couldn't wait."

"Just be thankful that we weren't in the middle of anything." Chambers grumbled as there was a rustling of sheets on his end. "My wife wouldn't be too impressed."

"Tell her I said I'm really sorry, but she knows I wouldn't call unless it was important."

Chambers grunted.

"That she does know. Give me a minute."

There were faint whispers at the other end, Chambers and a woman's voice. Emily silently groaned. God, she screwed that up. Now she wouldn't be able to get the image of Chambers in bed with his wife. That was certainly going to keep her up once everything else had died down.

A few moments later, there was the closing of a door and the creaking of a chair.

"Okay, I'm in my office now. I presume you're not calling with an update at this time of night, Lieutenant."

"No, I'm not." Emily pushed herself to her feet, toeing off her shoes. "Darryl Houghton-Leathers is here in Union. And he knows I'm here as well."

"What?" Now Chambers sounded less drowsy, his voice sharper. "How? Did you tell him?"

"Of course I didn't! Why would I do that?"

"I have to check, Emily. You were with him for a while."

"I didn't, sir! He's been stationed at Fort Jackson, and he wants to talk to me."

Chambers swore. He never cursed. Emily heard a thud at his end of the line.

"Colonel? What was that?"

"That was me throwing something. Now I've got a nice dent in the wall."

"Tracey's not going to like that."

"She doesn't come in here, so I'll get away with it." Chambers growled, the noise vibrating in Emily's ear. "Does he know where you work? Where you live?"

"He cornered me outside my work, so it's a safe bet he does. And unless he's followed me home, he won't know where I live for now."

Chambers hissed.

"This could be dangerous, especially if Marsden's on the run. I'll have a word with Houghton-Leathers' CO and see what I can do."

"Thank you."

Emily didn't know what to say other than that. She was too tired to care. Chambers sighed, barely hiding back a yawn.

"No need to thank me, Emily. You're one of my best."

"Nice to know you care."

"Don't talk rubbish. I want you back here and back to work. What is happening right now is just a blip."

"A blip that's lasted far too long already." Emily snorted.

Chambers grunted.

"I know. I'll see what I can do. Call me if anything else happens. Just not at a stupid time in the night."

"If you'd stuck me in the same time zone, it wouldn't be a problem to remember." Emily rubbed at her eyes. "I'll do my best, sir."

"Now, may I go back to bed?"

"Sure." Emily giggled. "You're going to need to make up a lot to Tracey now."

Chambers growled something rude before he hung up. Emily stared at the cell phone in her hand. Then she threw it across the hall, watching as it bounced off the wall before skittering away.

That didn't make her anger disappear. It was going to take more than that before she felt remotely better.

#

Six Months Later

Mike fumed as he sat in the back of the taxi, gritting his teeth as the driver tried to engage him in conversation. This felt like hell for him; Mike didn't do small talk. And the man just didn't understand that all his passenger wanted was for him to shut up.

If he found the person who damaged his jeep, Mike was going to string him up.

He had been in a good mood, even having to get up early to make sure Prudence got to school. She did plead for a lift, and Mike had been intending to do that, but then they had seen what had happened to his jeep. It had red paint thrown all over it, all the windows smashed, and the tyres were slashed. His car had been completely destroyed.

It had taken a moment before Mike realized that it wasn't red paint on his car, but blood. Pig's blood, hopefully; Mike didn't want to contemplate anything more than that.

Now Prudence had to head off for school, yawning as she got behind the wheel, and Mike had to make several calls. He was fuming. His carport was not visible from the road, and he was in a quiet suburb. How had someone managed to come in, vandalize his jeep, and gone again without anyone noticing? Mike had perimeter alarms, and they hadn't been tripped.

Carol had to be behind this. She knew about the alarms, and Mike had knocked her back again. It wouldn't be the first time she had done this; the woman had proven how vindictive she was.

If only Mike could prove that it was Carol. Each time something had happened where he needed to make a police report - his house had been broken into, manure had been dumped behind their cars, and now this - there was nothing to show for definite that it was Carol. Mike had wanted to say something, but accusing a woman of her stature of vandalism was never a good idea. Carol could sue for defamation of character, even if it was true.

Far too much hassle for him. Mike would rather just forget the woman existed.

Now everything was in motion. The police had looked it over and done their report, the jeep was being taken to the shop to see if it could be salvaged, and Mike had spoken to his insurance company. A replacement vehicle would be along later in the day to the restaurant.

But that didn't replace a vehicle he considered a prized possession. Even if his mechanic could fix his jeep, it wouldn't be the same as before. Mike didn't think that blood would come off so easily.

Carol was going to get a rude awakening once Mike managed to prove it was her. If not her, then someone she hired. She wasn't going to keep ruining things of his because she couldn't get her own way.

Finally, after what seemed like an age, the taxi arrived at Mike's restaurant. Thrusting wads of dollars into the driver's hand, Mike exited the car before it had barely stopped. Then he let out a heavy sigh of relief. He had a couple of hours before the restaurant opened, and it would be at least an hour of silence before anyone came in for work.

That hour of quiet Mike needed. Especially after the disaster with his car.

Mike was reaching into his pocket for his keys when a deep male voice behind him had Mike spinning around.

"Mike Wilson?"

A big, muscular man in his thirties with short blond hair wearing a suit that had seen better days walking across the parking lot. He easily topped six-five, his mouth thinned into a surly line. Even with the badge and gun clipped to his waistband, everything about him screamed cop.

"I am." Mike eyed him up and down. "And you are?"

The man tapped the badge at his waist.

"Detective Winston, Union PD."

"Union PD?" Mike arched an eyebrow. "I didn't think vandalism would be worthy of a detective."

"What are you talking about?"

"My jeep was vandalised this morning. Isn't that what you're going to talk to me about?"

Winston frowned and shook his head.

"No, I'm not here about that. This is much more serious."

Mike begged to differ on that. But he wasn't in the mood to argue.

"What is it?"

"Someone called 911 and said there was a break-in taking place at your restaurant."

"What?" Mike brought out his cell phone and checked it. No calls. "Nobody's called me about it. I've only just got here."

"Does anything look like it's been broken or smashed?"

Mike took a quick look over the back of the building. Everything looked in order.

"I don't think so, and the front looked okay. Perhaps it was a hoax call."

"Let's hope so. May I check the inside?"

Mike unlocked the door, stepping into the locker room and tapping in the code for the alarm. Then he took a quick glance around, heading into the kitchen. Nothing seemed to be out of place there. And there was nothing wrong with the downstairs bathroom or the larder. Mike tried to see if anything had been disturbed, but he couldn't.

Someone was playing games with the police.

"How many people work here?"

Mike turned to see Winston in the doorway. His frame seemed to loom in the space. Mike had to back up a couple of steps to see him properly.

"I have twenty people working for me, covering various shifts."

Mike headed through the locker room and into the kitchen. He could hear the footsteps of the detective following him. It was like being followed by a heavy-footed bullock.

"When do you open?" Winston asked as they entered the restaurant area.

"Half-eleven." Mike put his keys on the bar. "The staff working today won't turn up for another half-hour…"

That was when he saw the blood on the floor by the door to his office. The door was also partially open. It was never open of its own accord, the door too heavy to swing back and forth.

"Detective?"

"I see it." Winston took out his gun, signalling for Mike to stay back. "Stay here, Mr Wilson. I'll check it out."

"Like hell I am." Mike shot back hotly. "This is my business. I'm not going to stand back if someone's been trying to ruin it for me."

"Mr Wilson…"

Mike pushed past Winston, stepping over the blood as he shoved the door open with his shoulder. And then he saw the trail of blood going up the stairs, splattering on the tan-coloured carpet. Keeping to the side, Mike made his way up to the next floor, Winston following behind.

The trail went towards his office. Now the blood patches were bigger, as if something had been dragged. His heart pounding, Mike pressed a hand on his door and pushed it open slowly. The door snagged on the carpet, and Mike leaned on it. It opened suddenly, causing Mike to stumble into the room. He caught himself before landing flat on his face. Then he saw the scene before him.

There was a woman's body in his chair, seated behind his desk. She was slumped back, her throat slashed open. Mike could see that her eyes were open, staring sightlessly at the ceiling. Her blouse was sodden with blood, the blouse itself torn at one shoulder. Her red hair was matted and stuck together with the blood to her cheeks and forehead.

Mike had seen many deaths and many corpses. But this was something else. His stomach churned, and he had to look away. Behind him, Mike heard a muffled curse. Then Winston stepped past him, heading carefully around the blood and to the desk. Mike stared as the detective checked for a pulse, avoiding touching the wound.

"She's dead."

"I would be surprised if she managed to survive that."

"Do you recognize her, Mr Wilson?"

"No."

Mike watched as Winston picked up something from the desk, laid out in front of the body. It was a driver's license. Winston peered at the name.

"Her ID says her name is Karen Underwood. She's from Portland, Oregon."

"She's a long way from home." Mike mused.

Something caught his eye. On the floor by the filing cabinet was something metallic. Looking closer, it was a collection of metal tags on the end of a chain. They had a series of numbers and names that looked like gibberish, but Mike recognized them. He had a collection of his own at home.

Kneeling, Mike used a pen to pick the chain up.

"Look at this. Dog tags."

"Dog tags?" Winston straightened up. "The killer's?"

"I doubt it. They've got Underwood's initials on them." Mike stood, putting the tags on the desk. "She was a soldier."

"Are you sure you don't recognize her?"

"No, I don't." Mike sighed as he looked around the room. "I take it my office is going to be out of bounds."

"I'm afraid the whole building is out of bounds." Winston held up a hand as Mike started to protest. "You'll be lucky to conduct any business today. Not until we've processed the whole restaurant and its connecting rooms. And we'll need to talk to everyone who works here."

Mike wanted to protest, but wasn't going to get them anywhere. Winston was right. Someone had dumped a dead body in his place of business. Now they were standing in a crime scene. And Mike would have to take a step back and let the police take charge.

He hated doing that. Mike didn't like losing control. It was something he had gritted his teeth to during his army days. But he had also been taught to follow orders. That part of Mike won out. He squared his shoulders and took a deep breath.

"Okay, fine. But I can't afford to have more than just one day off if we're not able to get any custom today."

Winston arched an eyebrow.

"I would've thought with your business as prosperous as it was, you could afford to have a day off."

"In this current economic climate?" Mike snorted as he headed towards the door. "You must be joking."

Chapter Five

I t was going to be one of those days. Emily knew it. Another long shift with Mike present. Making Emily aware that he was there watching her.

Damn Callie. She had to go and tell Emily six months ago that Mike had a thing for her, didn't she? Much as Emily liked Callie, the woman was infuriating. She knew how to knock her off-balance. Especially when it came to men. Emily kept them firmly at arm's length for the time being. She didn't want to get to the point where she had to explain herself or disappear into thin air.

However, when it came to Mike...Emily didn't want to venture any further in that direction. The older man was far too tempting for his own good.

Emily needed to stay out of sight, not draw attention to herself. And yet she couldn't do it. Mike Wilson made her eager to show that she was there, even if Mike kept himself at a distance.

It had been seven months of working for him, seven months of dancing around each other, and Emily didn't know if she was able to continue with it. The tension was certainly building. It was going to explode soon. Emily could only hope that her predicament was tied up and sorted before it happened. Jumping into bed with someone before Marsden was caught would get someone else in the firing line.

Emily decided to give it another week. If Marsden hadn't been caught by then, she would disappear herself. Nobody, not even Chambers, would know where she had gone. She would go to the middle of nowhere and look after herself. The only person she could rely on was herself.

Emily was sharply jerked out of her thoughts when she saw the activity at the restaurant. It seemed like police cars were everywhere. There was a coroner's van just turning into the parking lot, and Emily could see a forensics truck by the back door.

What was going on? Had something happened to Mike? Emily's heart began to race at the thought. Mike was always the first one in, long before any of the staff turned up. Had he got into trouble? Had the place been burgled?

But that didn't explain the coroner's van.

No. Surely, Mike wasn't dead.

Emily parked haphazardly in an empty space at the far end of the lot and jumped out, absently grabbing her things. She half-walked, half-ran across the parking lot. The rest of the staff were hanging about nearby, clumped together with hurried whispers at each other.

Emily ignored her co-workers and went straight for the back door. Only to be blocked by an officer, who gave her a stern look and a shake of his head.

"Sorry, miss. You can't go in. This is a crime scene."

"But I work here." Emily protested, making her eyes wide. "What's happened?"

"I'm afraid I can't discuss that, miss." The officer gestured at her co-workers. "You're going to need to wait over there until the crime scene has been secured."

"But..."

Then Emily saw the gurney coming out, being pulled along by two men in white overalls. There was a body on top, zipped up to the neck. Long red hair poked out from the body bag, along with a whitened face, blood crusting on her cheeks and neck.

It took a moment for Emily to recognize her. Bile rose up in her stomach. *No. It couldn't be. What was she doing here?*

The officer growled and hurried inside, whispering furiously in one of the assistant's ears. They hurriedly zipped up the bagging, hiding the body from sight. Then they dragged the gurney out into the parking lot. A collective gasp came from Emily's co-workers, one of the other girls whimpering.

Someone started to cry. Emily couldn't respond. She was still staring at the body bag.

Not her. Surely not.

"Miss?"

Emily jumped when someone touched her arm. She looked up. The officer was at her side, looking down at her with a concerned frown on his brow.

"Hmm?"

"You look like you're about to faint."

"I..." Emily tried to collect herself for a response. She couldn't tell him the truth. She took a deep breath and squared her shoulders. "I've just not seen a dead body before."

The officer's expression softened.

"I understand." He paused and glanced towards the locker room. "I might get into trouble for this, but how about you go to the restroom? Take a few minutes in there."

That was more than Emily could have asked for. She gave him a small smile of thanks and stumbled inside. There wasn't anyone else in the locker room, leaving Emily's path uninterrupted. She entered the restroom and locked the door, her hands fumbling for her cell phone.

This was bad. Very bad. Emily dreaded to think what Chambers was going to think.

Her boss answered on the third ring. His voice was laced with amusement.

"I'm beginning to think you fancy me with the amount of times you keep calling me, Emily. At least you called me at a more sociable hour."

Emily pressed herself against the door, keeping her voice down to a whisper. She had no idea how long it would take before someone realized she was taking her time.

"Karen's dead."

"Karen?"

"Captain Underwood."

Chambers made a noise that sounded like a curse.

"How...how is that possible? She transferred to DC."

"Her body was at Wilson's restaurant."

"Are you sure?"

"I saw her myself."

Chambers cursed again. Emily had only ever heard him once like this and that was when he realized Emily had to go into hiding. It was a moment before Chambers could speak coherently again. He was breathing heavily.

"Any idea how she was killed?"

"Not yet. I only saw her face. She was coming out in a body bag."

"And she's not the only one."

"What do you mean?"

"I received notification about ten minutes ago from my contacts in DC." Chambers was practically snarling. "Samir Kashefi disappeared last week. We thought nothing of it due to his current work situation, but his body was found in a shallow grave just outside of DC."

Emily felt her legs give way. She sagged to the floor.

"Oh, God. No. Not Samir."

"He's been dead over a week." Chambers' voice softened. "I'm sorry, Emily."

Emily could feel the bile building in her throat. She pressed a hand to her mouth and tried not to throw up. Samir was a tough man who had a heart of gold. The guy was dedicated to his job. Emily could not fault him for that.

And now someone had killed him.

"What…" Emily tried to fight back the hysteria threatening to bubble up. "What does this mean?"

"It means that Marsden's getting close, and he has a list." Chambers said grimly. "You really need to go into a safe house, Emily. It's for your own protection."

"No. No, I won't."

"Emily…"

Emily shook her head.

"If he brought Karen here, the chances are he already knows where I am. He's going to know what's going on, and the safe house certainly won't be safe if he's watching me."

"We don't know where he is or how many people are involved with helping him." Chambers shot back sharply. "You know how slippery Marsden is."

"Sir, it's going to look suspicious if I disappear right now." Emily realized her voice was getting louder and she forced herself back down to a whisper. "The police are going to think I'm involved if I suddenly vanish."

"We'll figure it out. But I'm coming to Union. No arguments on that."

Emily didn't think she could argue on that. Chambers was just as stubborn as her, if not more so. She tugged her hand through her hair, tugging the bobble out and twisting it around her fingers.

"Oh, God." For the first time in months, Emily felt useless. "How am I going to explain this?"

"Like I said, we'll figure it out." Chambers' voice hardened. "I'm getting on a plane to Union. Sit tight. I'll be there soon."

He hung up before Emily could protest, and now all Emily could hear was the dial-tone. Much as she didn't want to feel like she was being mollycoddled, knowing that her boss was on the way made her feel a little better.

She jumped when there was a sudden banging on the door, almost dropping her phone. Then Emily heard Mike.

"Molly? Are you in there?"

Molly? Who's Molly? *It's you, you idiot. You're supposed to be Molly Ferrel, simple waitress. Nondescript.* Emily gritted her teeth and shoved her cell phone into her pocket.

"Just a second."

She flushed the toilet and then washed her hands, checking her hair in the mirror. It was loose, a mess about her shoulders, but that could be easily sorted. Taking a deep breath, Emily unlocked the door and opened it. Mike was standing in the doorway, his arms folded with a concerned frown creasing his forehead.

Emily managed a small smile at him, even as her heart sped up triple-time.

"Hey, Mike. Sorry, I didn't realize you needed to go."

"I didn't." Mike was still frowning. "What are you doing in there?"

"Do you need me to draw you a diagram?"

"That's not funny, Molly. I heard you talking to someone in there."

Emily silently cursed. She thought she hadn't been loud enough to be heard. *Remember, be the innocent, simple waitress.* Emily managed to summon up the tears, which came to her more easily than they should.

"I...I was on the phone to my dad."

"Your dad?" Mike blinked. "I thought you said your dad was dead."

Whoops.

"My stepdad. I just needed someone to calm me down." Emily swallowed, her stomach churning as she remembered Karen's expression and the deep wounds to her throat. Even after years on the job, she still hadn't got used to that. "I saw the body on the way out and...it freaked me out a bit."

That was the first most honest thing Emily had admitted to him. She didn't want to be considered as weak. Mike didn't appreciate weakness. Mike was still frowning at her. Then his expression softened. He reached out, rubbing her arm.

"I understand. It's never easy."

"You didn't see things like this in the army?"

"All the time. But it's not exactly something you can get used to."

His hand was warm. Very warm. Emily could feel it through her sweater. The heat was trickling up her arm. She bit her lip and tried to ignore it.

"Who was it?" She whispered. "Does anyone know?"

"We have a name, but I've never seen her before." Mike sighed. "Detective Winston is going to want to talk to everyone, so would you mind hanging around? I don't think we'll actually be working today, but the staff need to talk to the police."

Emily didn't want to stick around. She wanted to get out of there. Seeing Karen's body and knowing Samir had been killed had shaken her. She needed to regroup. But Emily couldn't deny Mike anything, even if everything in her wanted her to turn around and run.

"Sure. I'll do whatever I can to help."

Mike grunted. Then he seemed to realize that he was still touching Emily's arm and drew back abruptly, clearing his throat as his cheeks reddened.

"You go and join the others. I'll see what I can do here."

Emily wasn't about to argue. She averted her gaze and hurried out the back. It was only once she got out into the humid weather that Emily could breathe again. The longer she was around Mike Wilson, the more enticing he became.

She had never seen the appeal of forbidden fruit before. Now she understood.

#

Somehow, the police managed to get the crime scene processed and wrapped up by mid-afternoon. Just in time for Mike to set things up for the evening shift. While he didn't think working immediately after something like a murder was a good idea, it would certainly take his mind off things. From the reaction of his staff, they were thinking along the same lines. Everyone wanted to just get on with work and try to forget about the bloody body that had been up in Mike's office.

Even as he worked, Mike couldn't stop from looking over at Molly. She looked cool and collected, going on as normal. But there was a rigidness about her that was barely noticeable. She was scared about something and it was more than seeing a dead body.

What is she hiding?

Mike wanted to know. And he wouldn't get a straight answer from her. He would have to try another alternative method.

Leaving the bar, Mike slipped out into the parking lot. It was still very warm, but the air was cooling a little. The sun was a long way off setting, despite it being after seven. Mike moved to the far end of the parking lot and took out his cell phone. It had been a long time since he had used this number, but his old friend had made him promise to call if he needed any help.

And Mike certainly needed help now.

His call was answered on the second ring.

"Hello, Major Warden speaking."

Mike couldn't stop himself from smiling. Scott Warden was one of his squaddies from when they first enlisted. He had transferred to America a few years back. They were almost like brothers, although Scott was throwing himself more into his work after the death of his fiancée three years before. They hadn't spoken much since Mike had left, but their relationship never seemed to falter.

"Hey, bud. It's me."

"Mike!" Scott's surprise turned to genuine warmth. "Wow, it's been a while. How are you?"

"Muddling through. My knee's not packed up yet."

Scott chuckled.

"Well, that's something. You always were a stubborn bugger."

"No argument there."

"How's the restaurant? Is it still floating?"

"Yes, things are going well. Mostly." Mike winced. "Apart from today, that is."

"Oh, dear. Someone didn't pay their bill?"

"Not exactly." Mike couldn't stand still. He found himself pacing, even as his knee complained. "A dead body was found in my office today. A soldier."

There was silence for so long on the other end that Mike thought they had been cut off. Then Scott gave a low whistle.

"Whoa. I wasn't expecting that. What the fuck have you been up to?"

"Nothing, I swear."

"Well, you must've been up to something for this to happen."

"I didn't kill her."

"I never assumed...wait a minute, back up." Scott was now beginning to sound less friendly and more like the soldier he was. "Did you say 'her'?"

"Yes. Her name was Karen Underwood. Dog tags say she held the rank of Captain."

Mike jumped when he heard the sharp intake of breath at the other end. Scott's voice faded like he was in a daze and there was the sound of very heavy creaking. Scott must have sat down very heavily.

"Karen's dead?"

"Wait, you know her?"

"Of course I do. She's one of the soldiers who took a law degree and prosecuted corrupt squaddies for the MPs. She was originally at Fort Hood and moved to the west coast a while back. I've worked with her a few times."

That Mike hadn't been expecting. But at least he might be able to get an idea on why Karen Underwood was left with him.

"What was she like?"

"Solid, diligent and loyal. Good at her job. Great, even." Scott let out a heavy breath. "And you say she's dead?"

"I'm afraid so. I found the body."

"My God." There was an audible swallowing noise. "Shit. Her husband's going to be devastated. He works in the FBI field office in Houston."

"The police have more than likely contacted him, Scott. I'm sure they'll do the notification."

If Winston was thorough about it. Mike didn't have much to think about the detective in terms of his appearance, but he seemed to be pretty sharp when it came to his work. Hopefully, Karen's husband already knew about it. They would need a formal identification before they could go on with the autopsy.

There was a sound behind him that had Mike spinning around. But there was nobody in the parking lot. *Stop getting jumpy. The shadows will look like they're biting if you keep at it.*

"Hang on a minute." Scott's voice sharpened. "Did you say Karen was in Union?"

"Yes."

"That doesn't make sense. Karen wouldn't need to go over there. She's always elbows-deep in another case. In my experience, she was. Always on the go but never seemed to get anywhere, if you know what I mean."

"Been there, done that."

"What do you think it means if Karen was found there?"

Mike had been turning it over in his mind, but he was coming up with a lot of ideas and no substantial proof. It was just a mess. He rubbed his hand across his eyes with a heavy sigh.

"There's a connection between me and Karen Underwood. I just don't know what."

"And you want to know what I can dig up." Scott snorted. "I should have known you weren't calling to shoot the breeze."

"Scott, a dead body was left at my business. And I want to know why my business was made the final resting place."

Mike knew he wasn't in the army anymore, and this was asking for a lot. But he needed to know. He was not the sort of person who sat back and twiddled his thumbs while someone else did the work. Mike had to have an active role. He would be treading on Winston's toes, but Mike didn't care.

Scott sighed.

"I suppose I do owe you a lot. Ancient history and all."

"Thank you." Mike glanced back towards the restaurant. "Also, can you do some digging on someone else?"

"How many favours are you planning on cashing in?"

"Please, Scott."

Scott huffed.

"Okay, fine. Is this person a possible suspect?"

"One of my staff knows something about the dead woman, but I don't know what. I want to know if there's something more."

"That wasn't the answer to my question."

Mike hesitated.

"I don't think she's the killer. But she knows something, that much I'm certain about."

Scott grunted.

"I should've guessed it was a she. You always want to know about a woman."

"This is not funny, Scott."

"Okay, okay. Just give me her name. I'll see what I can dig up."

"Molly Ferrel." Mike spelled out the surname. "She says she's from Georgia."

There was the sound of scribbling.

"Got it. I'll look into those for you." Scott paused. "Stay safe, Mike."

Then Mike was listening to the dial-tone. Scott had never been very good at saying goodbye.

Mike put his cell phone away and made his way back into the restaurant. Molly was still working, taking orders from a family in a corner booth. She was smiling and glowing as she talked to the children. Mike felt a pang in his chest. Molly was so much as home working with children. It was completely natural.

Had she ever thought of becoming a mother?

Mike started. Where had that come from? Why was he thinking about Molly and children? He was very tired if he was starting to daydream of a white picket fence and all the trimmings.

He headed back behind the bar. There was a young man hanging around near the door, looking at all the faces in the restaurant area. Mike took an inventory of him, and immediately came up with 'soldier'. Dressed in denim jeans with a red shirt, African-American with a shaved head, the man had the demeanour of a squaddie. Mike knew the look in his eyes as well; he had seen it far too many times when he was in service.

Mike was already on the alert. What did he want? He cleared his throat.

"Can I help you, sir?"

The man started and looked around. They stared at each other, Mike noticing that the other man was looking decidedly twitchy. Then he approached the bar, flashing Mike an army ID badge.

"Sergeant Darryl Houghton-Leathers." He made it sound like it could get him anything. "I was looking for a friend. I wondered if she was working today."

"Well, I'm the boss. Who are you looking for?"

Houghton-Leathers hesitated.

"I...I was looking for Molly."

That had Mike stiffening. He knew Molly? She had never mentioned knowing a squaddie. And this one was looking as though someone was going to jump out at him.

His gut said this man was trouble.

"Molly's here, but she's working right now. She can't be disturbed."

"Just for a few minutes, surely?"

"No. We're behind today due to unforeseen circumstances. We can't afford to get further behind."

Houghton-Leathers' eyes narrowed. Now he was looking to go on the offensive. *Typical arrogant NCO type. They were just pathetic under that swagger.* Mike had no time for people like that.

"You're a hard ass, aren't you?"

"I don't let my staff fraternize with others when they're meant to be working. Money costs time."

Houghton-Leathers' jaw tightened. But he drew back, rapping his knuckles on the bar.

"Tell her Darryl wanted to see her." He ordered. "She knows how to get hold of me."

"Wait until she's off work before you talk to her." Mike shot back. "I'm not your messenger."

"I beg your pardon?" Houghton-Leathers leant back, hands on the bar. "Do you have any idea who I am?"

Mike had met arrogant men in the army before. This one was a pussycat compared to the others. He leant on the bar himself, inches away from Houghton-Leathers' face.

"You're a cocksure fool. I got to the rank of Sergeant Major before a landmine almost took my leg off. I took PT and drill for my base. I may be disabled, but I can wipe the floor with you, so don't even try it."

He saw the doubt flickering in Houghton-Leathers' eyes. Then the man's eyes narrowed again, looking Mike over like he was something he had just wiped off his shoe.

"Anyone would think you have a thing for Molly. Do you know the real person underneath? I bet you don't." He smirked and licked his lips. "I certainly know the real person."

Mike snarled.

"Get out."

"Fine, I'm going." Houghton-Leathers pushed back, looking smug. "But Molly isn't who you think. Delicious as she is, she's a liar, and I know it."

With a final smirk, Houghton-Leathers swaggered out of the door. Mike growled and grasped onto the bar, trying to control his breathing. That man was enough to make anyone lose their temper.

If Molly really knew him, it was a wonder Houghton-Leathers hadn't been killed already.

45

Chapter Six

The sound of his cell phone ringing shocked Mike out of his concentration. It was then he realized he had been sitting at his desk for most of the afternoon and evening, staring at a load of emails that were starting to blur together. His head was killing him.

So much for avoiding the rest of the staff to get on with work. To stop staring at Molly. Mike didn't think he had done anything. The clock said he had been there for three hours. He was vaguely aware of someone coming in, leaving the keys on his desk and bidding him goodnight, but Mike had no idea who had come in.

Molly was taking up his thoughts. A lot. And that wasn't good. Mike's strict rules were there for a reason. He wasn't supposed to break them, even if Prudence thought otherwise.

Then Mike realized it was Prudence ringing, her name flashing up on his cell phone. It stopped, showing that she had rung him five times already. Mike remembered they were supposed to be going to softball practise together. Mike always took his daughter and he went for a run while she practised with her team.

Cursing at himself, Mike picked up his phone just as it started ringing again.

"Prudence?"

"Who were you expecting to call? Are you okay, Dad? I've been calling you for three hours now."

Mike winced.

"Sorry about that. I completely forgot about everything else. And I forgot about softball practise."

"Don't worry, I got there and back. Although not for the lack of trying." Prudence sighed. "Someone slashed the tyres on my car."

"You what?" Mike sat up. "When did this happen?"

"While I was in school. They're looking at the security cameras to see if they can get anything, but I'm not holding much hope."

Mike closed his eyes. If this was Carol as well, she had gone too far going after his daughter. Mike would tolerate nothing if Prudence was targeted.

"Do not be surprised if you see Carol on the security cameras."

"You think she would sneak onto school grounds and mess with my car?"

That did sound odd, now Mike thought about it. Carol was a grown woman. Immature and didn't use her brain as often as she should, but she wasn't reckless. She wouldn't openly slash the tyres on her ex's daughter's car.

Wouldn't she?

"I'm sorry, Pru. I'll get things sorted with it as soon as I can."

"Don't worry, I've already done it. Your mate Jake picked it up ages ago." There was a rustling of papers and then Prudence spoke again. "Sorry, I was putting my feet up. They were falling asleep. Jeremy gave me a lift home and then offered to take me to softball practise. He does track close by, so it wasn't a problem to hitch a lift."

Jeremy? That had Mike sitting up. He hadn't heard about someone called Jeremy before. His protective side flared up.

"Who's Jeremy?"

"A guy in my class. He's been helping with chemistry."

"I see. And he's keeping his hands to himself, is he?"

Prudence burst out laughing.

"Not all the boys paw the girls, Dad. They certainly don't paw me. I think knowing I have a bruiser for a dad gives me some protection. No one wants to make a squaddie mad, ex-military or otherwise."

Mike blinked.

"A bruiser?"

"Well, you were a bit of a tearaway at school, weren't you?"

"I'm surprised you remember that."

47

"I may have been two years old when we moved to America, Dad, but I still remember the long walks and you pointing out your school. You even showed me the places you used to bunk off to."

Mike grimaced. He had forgotten how good children's memories could be, no matter how young they were.

His head was still hurting, and the ache was starting to increase behind his eyes. Mike leaned back in his chair and focused at a point on the wall, trying to relax his eyes. Even with his glasses on, it was still uncomfortable.

"He wasn't handsy with you, was he?"

"Jeremy? Of course he wasn't. Jeremy's sweet as anything."

"Just be careful with what you're doing. You don't want to give guys the wrong impression if they do a good thing for you."

Prudence was silent. Mike thought she had hung up. The silence was practically ringing in his ears.

"Prudence?"

"Dad, will you just give over."

"What? What have I done now?"

"I'm eighteen now. I am capable of being sensible. You seem to forget that at times. I can take care of myself."

Mike winced. His daughter's telling off was making his headache worse.

"I'm sorry, Prudence. I guess I still look at you and see the little girl I came back to."

Prudence sighed.

"With the horrors in your life, I don't blame you. And when I heard the news about what happened at your restaurant, I figured you would be busy. Jeremy was more than happy to drive me home."

That had Mike sitting up. He had been so engrossed in trying to distract himself from the gorgeous waitress downstairs that he had almost forgotten a dead body had been sitting in his chair. He stood up hurriedly, trying to look at his backside to see if there was any blood. There was nothing and it was a different chair with the old one having been taken away for analysis, but Mike didn't feel comfortable.

He needed to get a new chair. Maybe rearrange the room a bit. Then he wouldn't walk in and envision the dead squaddie each time.

"Dad? You still there?"

"I'm still here." Mike sat on the couch instead, rubbing at his head. Where were those aspirin when he needed them? "I haven't checked the news today. What did they say?"

"All they said was that a woman was found dead in your restaurant. They didn't say it was one of the staff or anything."

"It wasn't one of mine, don't worry."

Prudence grew silent. Then she swore loudly.

"Bloody hell."

"Prudence!"

"What? I'm an adult now."

"What's with the cursing, though?" Mike rubbed his ear. "And into my lug-hole as well?"

"Sorry. I just realized. You found her, didn't you?"

"How did you guess?"

"The tone of your voice. It's that same one that you used to have when you called home. Haunted." Prudence's voice softened. "I'm sorry you had to go through that, Dad."

Mike's chest tightened. He had tried to keep everything away from his daughter, but not quite. She was very astute.

"Thanks, honey." He lay down on the couch, stretching his legs on the cushions as he smiled. "So, when is Jeremy taking you out for that date?"

"What?" Prudence squeaked. "How do you know he asked me out?"

Mike laughed.

"I know you, Prudence. There's something telling me that says you were asked. And you're a pretty girl. If you weren't asked out, I'd be very surprised."

"Dad! You make it sound like I go running around with everyone."

"Not quite, but close enough."

Prudence snorted.

"Meanie. Anyway, Jeremy wants to take me out on Saturday to go bowling."

"Bowling." Mike sniggered. "Help you with your technique?"

"Dad, stop!"

"Sorry. But you don't need my permission, remember? You're eighteen."

"I'm just letting you know as a courtesy. I live in your house. I don't want the door locked on me."

"Knowing you, you'll be able to get in somehow."

Then Mike heard some shouting. It sounded like it was coming from the parking lot. He sat up, tossing his glasses onto the desk, and hurried over to the window overlooking the lot. There were two people struggling beside a car. One very big and dressed in black. The other was slight. Mike couldn't see who it was, but then he saw the flash of red hair.

Molly.

"I've got to go, Prudence."

"Okay. Be careful getting home."

"Will do. Love you."

Mike hung up and tossed his cell phone onto the couch. Then he reached underneath it and found his gun, sliding it out the holster. It had been a while since he had thought it would actually come in use.

#

Emily was exhausted. She was looking forward to going home and sliding into her warm bed. Everything else could wait.

Knowing that Karen and Samir were dead had shaken her. Emily had thought her lucky escape was bad enough, that she was the only target. Now it looked like the rest of them were on the hit list.

Marsden was really out for blood.

Emily knew, deep down, that she had to get out of there. Chambers was going to be in Union in the morning, and she would finally agree to going into a safe house. Everyone around her was going to become collateral damage. Marsden wouldn't care who he hurt as long as he got his own back on the people who took away his control, his source of income. Especially when Darryl knew where she was and had come into the restaurant after Emily told him to keep away. That was far too dangerous.

But leaving now would look suspicious. Particularly when Mike was keeping a close eye on her. He suspected something, and Emily knew he would be close to figuring out that Karen was linked to her. Mike Wilson wasn't stupid, and he had his contacts. All soldiers, past and present, had the right sources when they needed something.

Chambers would be furious about it. They had chosen Mike as Emily's boss due to their soldier connections, but Emily guessed that Chambers hadn't expected Mike to be smarter than they thought. He had overestimated the former squaddie.

Emily certainly had. She hadn't expected the man to get under her skin so easily. She had come into contact with many handsome men in her work. The majority of soldiers exuded an appeal that had women draping themselves all over them. But it had never affected her.

Until now. Even Mike's limp was downright sexy.

She had to stop thinking about him. Things were already messy. Emily couldn't afford it to get even worse.

Her feet were sore and throbbing as Emily crossed the parking lot. Being on her feet all day was something she could handle, but running around like this, getting toes squished by chairs and unruly customers, made them swell up. Emily had a newfound respect for waitresses after being in their shoes for seven months.

Emily had dropped the keys off in Mike's office before she left, but Mike had been glued to his computer, his glasses sat firmly on his nose. He had barely acknowledged her, but Emily had seen the faraway look in his eyes. She could relate. A lot.

Maybe a couple of days away from him could get Emily's head clear. She highly doubted it, but one could hope. She would put in for some time off soon. Then she would disappear under the radar.

Emily was almost at her car when she heard something behind her. She spun around. It was dark, but Emily's eyes scanned the parking lot. There was nobody there, and the silence was beginning to deafen her.

Not relaxing, Emily reached into her bag and drew out her mace. She could feel shivers go up her spine. It could be nothing, but she was feeling very jumpy right now.

Then someone came out of nowhere, slamming into her. Emily was knocked against a nearby car, pain shooting up her hip. Emily felt hands clamping down over her fingers, forcing the mace out of her hands. She reacted without thinking, kicking out. Her foot connected with a knee, and she heard a grunt. Then Emily managed to get one hand free. She punched her assailant in the throat.

He gurgled and clutched at his throat, letting go of her. Her mace was sent spinning across the ground, disappearing under another car.

Emily punched her attacker in the stomach before driving her forearm into him, her elbow catching him under his rib cage. Then she grabbed his shoulders and brought him down. Her knee connected with his face and his head jerked back before he went down, hitting the ground with a loud smack. Then he was kicking out, grabbing at her legs.

Emily managed to dance out of the way and ran. If she could get to her car, maybe she could find safety inside and get out of there.

She was tackled from behind, the weight making Emily's legs buckle. They landed in a heap on the concrete. Pain shot through her hands and knees, the heavy weight pressing her down. Emily gasped as her wrist threatened to snap.

Then an arm looped around her throat and began to squeeze. Emily struggled, but she couldn't move. Black spots were starting to appear in front of her eyes. Emily tried to wriggle her chin down to get a bite out of the arm, but it pressed in tighter.

"Hey!"

Emily was aware of a shout from somewhere above her. Then there was the sound of gunfire. Emily heard a muffled curse above her before she was let go abruptly. She sprawled on the ground as the heavy weight came off her and disappeared, air coming back into her lungs far too fast.

Through her haze, the world tilting sideways, Emily could hear running footsteps, more gunfire. Then silence. Emily tried to get up, but her head spun too much, and she had to slump back on the ground down again.

"Molly!"

Footsteps got louder, and then someone was kneeling beside her, urging Emily onto her side. A hand stroked her head, brushing her hair aside.

"Molly? Look at me, honey."

Honey. When was the last time someone called you that?

It took a moment for her vision to clear, and Emily saw Mike looking down at her. His hands were very cool on her hot skin.

"Mike?"

"Are you okay?" Mike winced. "Sorry. Stupid question."

"I'm fine." No, she wasn't. Emily's throat was sore, and her wrist was throbbing badly. "My head hurts, though."

Mike hesitated. Then he drew Emily to a sitting position, cradling her against his chest. Emily was so stunned she could barely move. Mike had been gentle before, on very rare occasions, but never like this.

She didn't want to leave his embrace.

Then Mike was helping her to her feet, still holding her against him.

"Come on. We're going back inside."

Back inside. She couldn't. Emily tried to pull away.

"I can't. Just let me go home, Mike."

But Mike's embrace tightened around her.

"Not a chance."

Chapter Seven

Mike's heart was still going a hundred miles an hour as he drew Molly back to the restaurant, urging her back inside despite her obvious intentions to run. Seeing her in a chokehold had made his heart stop before shooting into overdrive. If he hadn't heard the altercation, he wouldn't have come upon them.

Molly leaned against him as they entered the main dining area, Mike helping her towards a table. She was trembling, and her body felt hot. She was sweating. Mike had a feeling she was more hurt than she was willing to admit. Molly was tough, but this was not the time to push help away.

Selfishly, Mike wanted Molly to want him.

Later. Focus on that later. If it ever happens.

Mike got Molly to sit down before kneeling before her. Then he took her hands, turning them palm-up. Both of them had bloody scrapes.

"That looks painful. We'll get you cleaned up."

"I'm okay." Even as she said it, Molly didn't pull her hands away. "It's nothing."

"Don't argue with me, Molly."

Molly fell silent, but her eyes were bright. It was dim in the restaurant, but Mike was sure that her eyes were dilating. Was his closeness affecting her? Clearing his throat, Mike stood and hurried behind the bar, fetching the first aid kit. Then he was back in front of Molly, cleaning her hands.

It was hard not to think about how close he was to her right now.

Once her hands were cleaned, and Molly's skin was looking bright pink instead of red and bloody, Mike disposed of the wipes and put the first aid kit away. When he came back, Mike leaned over Molly as she sat. She was trying not to look at him. Putting his fingers under her chin, he lifted her face gently to him, hearing the sudden hitch in her breathing as he reached up and began to gently probe his fingers over her scalp.

"What are you doing?"

"I'm checking your head."

"Mike, I…"

"What did I say?"

Molly pursed her lips.

"Don't argue with you."

"Good girl."

He did the usual checks for a concussion. Molly followed his instructions easily enough, looking very alert. She wasn't showing signs of any concussion, which was a relief.

"Well, there doesn't seem to be anything wrong with your head."

Molly grunted.

"I've got a hard head. People have commented on it before."

"I'm sure they have."

Then Molly pulled her head back. She stood, turning away from him and started to look around the table.

"What are you looking for?"

"My bag. I need to get out of here."

Mike had dropped it back in the locker room, but he wasn't about to tell Molly that. He wanted answers.

"No, you're not going anywhere."

"What?" Molly spun around, her eyes narrowing. "What does that mean?"

"I'm not letting you out of here until you tell me what the hell's going on."

Now Molly really looked like she was about to run. Mike moved until he was blocking her exit. The front doors were locked, and the only way out was out the back. Molly would have to get past him.

Then Molly huffed and stomped over to him, trying to push him out the way. Mike didn't budge, but he was surprised at Molly's strength as she shoved his hands against her chest. She could give as good as she got.

Damn, if that wasn't arousing.

"I'm not telling you anything." Molly snapped. "And you can't keep me hostage over it. It's none of your business."

"None of my business, is it?"

Mike grabbed her around the waist and hauled her against him. Molly fell against his chest, her hands splaying across his shirt. Mike could feel the heat from her fingertips. For a moment, his lust surged to the surface, and he wanted to kiss her, take that mouth as he had wanted to for a long time. But Mike shoved that back down, cupping the back of Molly's head as he made her look at him.

"It became my business when you came to work for me." He hissed. "I make sure to take care of my staff. And I'm not about to walk away because you want me to. That's not my style."

Molly's mouth opened and closed. Mike didn't think he had ever seen her speechless. Then her jaw tightened.

"You're going to have to." She was making no effort to leave his arms. "I can't afford for anyone else to get hurt."

"That was my bread and butter at one point."

"And until a year ago, it was mine. I get that." Molly swallowed. "But if you get involved, you'll get pulled into more than you bargained for."

Now Mike was confused. *What did that mean? Did she just say...?*

"What was your bread and butter?" He narrowed his eyes. "Are you a soldier, too?"

Molly closed her eyes. Then she let out a heavy sigh, resting her forehead against his chest. The feel of her leaning on him again had all the blood rushing out of Mike's head. Goddammit, this was not the time to start thinking about getting Molly on the table and doing whatever he wanted to her.

Get a grip, you idiot.

"My boss is going to chew me out for this." She mumbled.

"Molly, what's going on? Tell me what you mean."

Molly lifted her head.

"If I tell you, will you give me back my bag and let me go?"

"I'm not promising anything unless you tell me."

Molly looked like she wanted to run. On instinct, Mike's arms tightened around her. It felt very good holding her close. Heat warmed his belly, and Mike knew his thoughts weren't going to be a secret for much longer. Not if he kept holding Molly like this. His cock was certainly going to be broadcasting a very clear message.

When Molly did speak, her voice changed. She sounded different, almost resigned.

"My name isn't Molly Ferrel. I took that on a few months ago." Molly briefly closed her eyes, and then she opened them. "My real name is Emily O'Rourke. I'm a Lieutenant in the military police force, stationed at Joint Base Lewis-Mcchord."

#

Emily saw the shock pass across Mike's face. He looked like someone had hit him over the head. She felt his arms loosen, and Emily took that chance to step out of his embrace, backing out of reach. She could think more clearly when Mike wasn't touching her.

Especially when she could feel his hardness pressing into her belly. It had almost made her lose the ability to speak. Emily needed to get out of his arms and not think about pressing closer to see how hard he really was.

Stop it. He was out of bounds before and he's certainly out of bounds now.

"You're...you're an MP?"

Mike sounded dazed. Emily bit her lip and nodded.

"Yes."

Mike's mouth opened and closed, but no sound came out. Emily had never seen him speechless before. Then Mike cleared his throat and shook himself, narrowing his eyes at her.

"And why are you here? Am I under observation or something? Because I've never been charged with anything in my life."

Emily sighed.

"This is not about you, Mike. Don't get in such a flap." She rubbed her hands over her face. "This is about me."

She had to stop talking. Chambers was going to have her head for saying anything. When they had decided Emily was to go into hiding, she knew that everything had to be kept a secret, that nobody was to know, or they would be considered a target as well. That was the point of being in hiding.

She should have knocked Mike out and run, taken her chances elsewhere. But Emily couldn't bring herself to do it. Not with Mike.

Never with Mike Wilson.

"Well?"

Emily jumped. Mike was still watching her, reminding her of a hawk eyeing up its prey before it swooped down. It sent a shiver up her spine, heat spreading through her belly. The man had a frustrating effect on her, one that Emily couldn't afford to deal with right now.

"Well, what?"

"Are you going to tell me what's going on?"

"You..." Emily shook her head. "No, Mike. Don't."

"Why not? A dead soldier was found in my office – which I'm guessing is associated with you – and you have another soldier asking questions..."

"Darryl." Emily kicked at a nearby table, making it slide across the floor. She wished it was Darrl's head. "I told him not to come here, but he wouldn't fucking listen."

"You know him?"

"Unfortunately." Emily winced when she saw Mike's outraged expression. "But I can't explain it. Please, don't ask me to. You know the game."

"I may know the game, but you just dragged me into it." Mike folded his arms. He was still scowling. "You're going to have to explain yourself, Molly...Emily."

Damn, that felt good hearing him finally say her name.

"This is nothing to do with you, Mike."

"It became something to do with me when it started coming into my business." Mike shot back. "You're not getting out of this. You tell me what the fuck's going on."

Emily wanted to go back to her apartment. Her head hurt, her wrists hurt, her hands were stinging, and she was feeling sick. But Mike wasn't going to let her leave. Not willingly, anyway.

But she couldn't say anything. Not just yet. Or Chambers really would have her head.

She pretended to sway, pressing her hands to her head.

"I need to go home." She said. "I feel sick."

Mike looked like he didn't believe her. But he nodded grimly and fished out the keys from his pocket.

"Then wait while I get my things. I'm taking you home."

"No!" Emily tried to protest. "I can…"

"If you've just been attacked, you can't drive. You shouldn't be behind a wheel. Not with the way you're holding your wrist against your chest."

Emily looked down. Sure enough, she was holding her injured arm against her. She hadn't realized she was doing that. Mike glared at her.

"I'm driving you home. No arguments, Emily."

This was not good. Emily could not let him take her back. He wouldn't leave. But he wasn't going to let her leave alone.

The man was too infuriating for his own good. And she was in big trouble.

Chapter Eight

Emily huddled in the passenger seat, watching Mike as he drove them back to her apartment. Damn, he was very insistent on that. Emily couldn't dissuade him from escorting her back. And, if she was honest, she didn't want to be alone right now.

Although this silence was very uncomfortable. Mike was clearly still digesting what little Emily had told him. She could see the range of emotions passing across his face, mostly confusion. A bit of anger. A lot of genuine surprise. She couldn't blame him for being shocked. Emily just wished he would back away and leave her be.

The bastard was just very stubborn.

Emily rubbed her arms, wishing she had put her sweater on and not stuffed it in her bag.

"Mike?"

"Hmm?"

Mike didn't look at her, his eyes firmly on the road. His knuckles were white on the steering wheel. Emily bit her lip.

"You okay?"

"How am I supposed to answer that?"

Emily winced.

"I'm sorry. But this was not something I could disclose."

Mike growled. Emily was half-expecting him to bare his teeth.

"I still should have been told." He snapped. "You were under my roof, working for me. I should have been notified."

"Come on, Mike, you know how it works. It was for my protection."

And Mike's as well. If it had been discovered by Marsden that Mike had been willingly harbouring his target, Mike would have been in the firing line as well. He was a civilian now, and Emily wasn't prepared to get anyone else involved.

Too late.

"Can I ask you something and get an honest answer?"

Emily swallowed. She was still getting goosebumps along her arms at the sound of his voice. Not the most appropriate of times to be aroused.

"I'll do my best."

"I suppose I asked for that." Mike grunted. He stopped at the intersection, but he still didn't look at her. "Is the fact I'm ex-army the reason you came to work for me?"

That was a safe question. Reasonably. Emily relaxed.

"Partly. My bosses sourced you out. And partly because they wanted me to do something that wouldn't draw attention to myself."

"So, you became a waitress." A small smile tugged at Mike's mouth. "That is a downward career move if ever I heard one."

"Really?" Emily shot back. "What do you call what you do for a living?"

"I opened a bar, and then a restaurant. I'm the owner, not a waiter."

Emily snorted.

"You're definitely not a waiter. You haven't got the patience."

"Neither have you."

"I'm good at hiding it."

Mike gave her a sidelong glance. The look in his eyes had Emily shivering. Even angry, he still had an effect on her.

Focus, Emily. Focus. Just not on him.

"Not with me." Mike murmured.

Emily squared her shoulders, glaring at him. He wasn't going to get her into a quivering mess. *Too late.*

"You know me that well, do you?" She challenged.

Mike sighed. He turned away and put the car into gear as the lights turned green.

"I thought I did."

Emily had nothing to say to that. She sat back as the car started moving again, pressing herself closer to the door. The tension in the car was thickening, and it was getting uncomfortably warm, whereas moments before it had been cold. The silence was deafening, and Emily could feel it ringing in her ears.

Why didn't she take Chambers' suggestion to go straight into a safe house in the middle of nowhere? Why did she have to hide in plain sight?

All Emily could hope for was that Mike walked away. Too many people she cared about had died over this already. Emily didn't want Mike to become the next one.

After what felt like forever, the minutes dragging by, Mike pulled up outside Emily's building. Emily fumbled with her seatbelt in her haste to leave.

"Thanks for taking me home." She reached for the door handle. "I can do it by myself now."

Then she tried the door. It wouldn't budge. Emily tried to open it again, but it wouldn't move. She glared at Mike, who was still staring out the front.

"Could you unlock the door now?"

"I can't do that." Mike turned to look at her. "Not unless I come up with you."

"You what?"

"Molly…" Mike winced. "Emily…fuck, that's going to take some getting used to…you were attacked tonight. I like to think of myself as a gentleman. So I want to make sure you get to your apartment without anything else happening."

Emily felt her pulse stumble for a moment. When was the last time she had someone act a gentleman with her? She was normally so determined to be independent and didn't need anyone to be her knight in shining armour. Her ex-boyfriend had known that and backed away. He didn't even try. So why did the thought of Mike doing it have her all of a flutter?

Because you know he's going to be in your apartment. Close quarters. Shit.

"I…" Emily squeaked. She cleared her throat. "I can take care of myself."

"And how did that go for you earlier?"

Emily could tell he wasn't going to back down. Huffing, she threw her hands up.

"Fine. You can walk me up. Don't expect a kiss goodnight."

"Eh?"

Emily didn't answer. Her face getting warm, she turned away and jumped out the car as soon as she heard the locks coming off. Why had she felt the need to say that? Her brain hadn't caught up with her mouth, something Emily was guilty of many times over. She really needed to watch what she was saying.

And what you're doing. Don't paw the man like you wanted to earlier.

She hurried towards her apartment building, aware of Mike's footsteps behind her. If only Emily had refused his offer to walk her up. But then he wouldn't have let her out of the car. All she could hope for was to get into her apartment as quickly as possible and lock the doors.

The elevator was out of order, which had Emily groaning. That would happen on a night like this. They had to take the stairs. *Shit.* But knowing Mike was behind her, agonizingly close, had Emily climbing the stairs. Her muscles were screaming at her, and Emily wanted to sit down, but she kept going.

They reached her floor. Emily's apartment was directly opposite the stairs. As they reached the landing, Mike was suddenly at Emily's side and grabbing her arm.

"Slow up." He nodded at Emily's door. "What's that?"

Emily looked. Then she noticed the note pinned to her door. She sighed.

"It's probably the caretaker again. He's been leaving notes all week. We've had a lot of maintenance on the building lately and he never seems to catch me."

Mike frowned at her. Stepping past her, he snatched the note off the door and scanned it.

"You sure about that?"

"Why?"

"Because this is a threatening note. 'You were lucky. Not next time'. Unless the caretaker has a grudge against you for a leaky pipe, chances are it's the same person who attacked you earlier tonight."

Emily suddenly felt cold. She snatched the note from his hand and looked over it. It wasn't a note from the caretaker and Mike wasn't taking rubbish. She groaned and scrunched the note in her fist.

"Oh, great. Now my cover's really been blown."

"We don't know that yet." Mike shoved his hands into his pockets. "But you need to notify your bosses."

Emily wasn't looking forward to that conversation.

#

Emily prided herself on keeping her place clean. She was used to smaller spaces. After serving overseas twice, keeping her belongings to a minimum was second-nature. She was not a materialistic person, and it was so much easier not to become too attached. But there was something about letting someone else into her own personal space. It was a space where she was supposed to feel safe.

And with Mike Wilson about, Emily did not feel safe at all.

She kicked off her shoes as Mike stood in the middle of the lounge, turning in a slow circle. Emily saw a slight smile twitching at his mouth. She bristled; she didn't want a remark about her living arrangements right now.

"It's not as big as my place in Tacoma." She said defensively.

"I wasn't going to say anything."

"You looked like you were about to."

Mike turned to her. He was still smiling, and Emily wished that he wouldn't. Far too handsome for his own good. The air practically sizzled around him. She should have refused him access up to her apartment. The place was too small, and even across the room he felt far too close.

"I was about to say nice place. Better than my home." Mike shrugged. "Then again, I live with my daughter and she's a teenager. Not the tidiest of people."

"I can imagine." Emily mumbled. She edged towards the bedroom. "I need to call my boss."

"I'll be in the kitchen."

Emily watched him stride towards the door, heading into the kitchen. She wanted him to leave as much as she wanted him to stay. The damn man had no idea what he was doing to her.

Or maybe he did and he was fucking with her. She was in deep trouble if he did know.

She had to stay focused. Shutting the door to her bedroom, resisting the urge to slam it, Emily fumbled for her cell phone. Chambers answered on the second ring with a hint of amusement in his voice.

"I'm getting flattered with the attention you're giving me, Emily, but my wife is going to think something else is going on."

"Are you on your way here?"

"I'm at the airport waiting to board. Providing there aren't any problems, I'll be in Union about seven in the morning your time. Why?"

Emily sagged onto the bed.

"I was attacked tonight."

The amusement disappeared. And now Chambers sounded like the man Emily was used to as his toner sharpened. And it still made her sit up straight.

"Where did this happen?"

"In the parking lot outside work."

"Any damage?"

Emily shook her head. Her throat was feeling tender and her head was pounding. Shaking it just made it worse.

"I'm more shaken than anything." She lied. "Mike Wilson took me home. We found a threatening note on my door. Sir, I think my cover's been blown."

Chambers was silent. Emily checked her phone, and they were still connected. Then as she put her phone back to her ear, Chambers let out a loud curse that made Emily almost drop the phone.

"Sir! Let me know when you're going to do that!"

"Screw that." Chambers muttered. "Where are you now?"

"In my apartment, with the door locked." Emily paused. " Wilson is here as well. He...he knows I'm not Molly Ferrel."

The curse that came from her boss was even louder. Emily flinched and rubbed her ear.

"Stop doing that!"

"What the hell did you tell him for? He wasn't supposed to be made aware of this!"

"I didn't have a choice. He wouldn't let me leave without an explanation. And he did rescue me." Emily squared her shoulders. "I need to choose people I can trust to be around me."

"And you trust Wilson, do you?"

"I do."

Emily didn't need to think about it. She had already made her mind up. Chambers snorted.

"Well, that remains to be seen. Don't tell him anymore about anything until I've had him checked out."

"Didn't you do that when I went to work for him?"

"Don't play smart with me, Emily. I need to know he won't sell you out."

"He won't."

She had known Mike long enough to know he wouldn't sell her out. He was as solid and as loyal as you could get anyone. Emily admired loyalty in a person, and Mike's was steadfast. That man would not let you down once he was on your side.

You want more than loyalty from him, though. Like what he was hiding in his pants earlier.

Shut up.

"Emily?"

"Hmm?"

"I'm just boarding the plane right now. I'll be in Union soon." Chambers' voice softened. "Sit tight, Lieutenant. It won't be long."

"You have my address, Sir."

Emily hung up. She sat on her bed and stared at the floor. This was not what she had expected. Not at all. She had expected Marsden to try and find her, but Emily had thought she was smarter than that. She could always stay one step ahead.

Ever since Marsden had got into her home and tried to kill her, Emily had thought she had been able to do that. But not anymore.

Now Marsden was practically on her doorstep and Emily was scared. Very scared. And she hated it.

Chapter Nine

Mike flicked the kettle on and pressed his hands to the counter, trying to slow his breathing. His heart had been racing all the way back to Emily's place, Mike believing that every vehicle that passed them or followed them for longer than was comfortable carried someone who wanted Emily harmed.

Or killed.

It had to be the latter. Emily wouldn't have ended up in hiding if there was no real threat on her life. And whoever it was had to have deep pockets. A fellow soldier with connections in the underworld? That wouldn't be a surprise. It had happened many times before and Mike had witnessed one or two. Squaddies wanted a bit more cash and the lure of more money than they knew what to do with tempted even the toughest of soldiers. Mike had never been tempted, but some people he had once called friends had.

Emily was military intelligence. An elite department in the military police. She would be investigating her own people on another level to simply dealing with aggressive jarheads who had had one beer too many and thought they were Sylvester Stallone. These people Emily would go after were the more dangerous ones. Those who would kill their friends if it meant they got more money.

And now one of them was after Emily.

She would now have to go into a safe house, off the grid completely, until whoever it was going after her had either been caught and was back in jail or dead. Mike shuddered. As long as Emily wasn't dead, that was fine by him.

It was the most sensible solution. But Mike didn't like it. He didn't like the thought of Emily being the target of a criminal who thought he could make all his problems go away by getting rid of her. He had a sudden urge to grab Emily and take her as far away as possible, anywhere, as long as he was with her.

As if you're going to let her out of your sight now this has happened.

Mike closed his eyes and took a deep breath. And again. He could not think with the wrong head right now. His desires needed to be put on the back seat. Emily's safety was more important than his need to have her in his bed, preferably naked and wrapped around him.

She was young enough to be his daughter. Emily might have been a grown woman - and a damn beautiful one - but that age gap alone should have been enough to make Mike back off. It didn't. And that was concerning. Mike should have been saying this was bad, and he had at the start. When the attraction first stirred, it had left Mike shaken. Emily was barely out of her mid-twenties. He was fifty. It made him feel like a pervert.

Now as the months passed, he was beginning to ignore that. He didn't care anymore. Emily was a single woman, and he was a single man. For the first time in his life, he had been considering breaking his own rule about not sleeping with his staff.

Give it a couple more days and you might have had her where you wanted her. And then this had to happen.

His cell phone bleeped, and then Mike remembered his daughter. Damn, he needed to stop forgetting that he was a father, even if said daughter would easily look after herself. He fished out his phone and dialled for Prudence. His kid answered on the second ring.

"Hey, Dad."

"Hey, kid." Mike glanced at the time. "Why are you still up?"

Prudence laughed.

"Dad, it's Friday night. I don't have classes on Saturday, or any games. I'm just here with Colette chilling to some movies. We're going to have a sleepover."

"Nice of you to let me know you were having a sleepover."

"I wasn't going to, but after what happened with you at work and with our cars, I didn't want to wait until you got home. Colette said she would stay over to keep me company." There was a muffled voice. "She says hi, by the way."

"Hi back." At least his daughter wasn't alone. That did make Mike feel a little better. "Actually, I was going to let you know I wouldn't be home tonight. So just set the alarm when you go to bed if you haven't already."

"Not yet. I was waiting for you." Now Prudence was sounding concerned. "What's the matter, Dad? What's happened?"

"One of my waitresses was attacked this evening. I'm staying at hers just to make sure she's okay."

That was the truth, certainly. But as much as Mike was prepared to say to his daughter. He had already dragged himself into Emily's problems, and there was no way he would do the same to Prudence.

"Someone got attacked." Prudence said slowly.

"That's what I just said."

"Is the waitress you're with Molly, by any chance?"

"Huh?" It took a moment for Mike to remember that Molly was Emily. God, he was going to get his mind twisted trying to get the name right. "Why do you say that?"

"Because there's a certain waitress you're hot for and you wouldn't stay the night to make sure for anyone else." Prudence sniggered. "Dad, why don't you say you're going to sleep with her and you'll be having so much fun you won't want to come home? I'm a big girl."

"I'm serious, Prudence." Although Mike knew his face was going red. Thank God his daughter couldn't see him. "Molly was badly hurt. I want to know she's okay."

"Yeah, keep telling yourself that, Dad." Prudence laughed. "Look, don't worry about me. I'll text you when I go to bed, and Colette's with me. You don't have to focus on me."

"Force of habit, Pru. You're my kid. Don't expect me to get out of over-protective mode that quickly."

"I know." Prudence's voice softened. "I love you, Dad. Stay safe. And night."

"Night. And love you, too."

Mike hung up, and then checked the kettle. It had boiled, Mike almost burning his fingers off as he pressed them against the appliance. He looked around and found some cups in a cupboard. It was the middle of August and very hot, but he found a cup of tea always calmed someone down. It had to be the British in him.

Hopefully, Molly - Emily - had some around, and then he could see about getting her calm enough to sleep. Alone.

But for how much longer?

#

Emily couldn't breathe. It felt like someone was sitting on her chest. She tried to push it off, but it wouldn't budge. Then she was there, in her old home. In her bed.

And Marsden was in the doorway.

Emily went for her gun, but Marsden got there first, snatching it out of her hand. He hit her hard, several times. Emily tried to fight back, but she was trapped under the duvet, pinned down by Marsden's weight as he jumped on her.

Then his hands were around her throat and squeezing. Emily tried to scream, but no sound came out. She was unable to move as everything started going black, unable to breathe. Things were going hazy. Marsden's smug sneer became blurred. But this time, no one was there to save her. Emily tried to scream again, but she couldn't. She was falling, falling, and she still couldn't breathe.

"Emily! Wake up!"

What? That wasn't part of her nightmare. And the hands weren't at her throat anymore. They were shaking her by the shoulders, jerking her back from her falling.

Emily felt the air rush back into her lungs and she woke up gasping, clawing her way back out of the blackness. The feel of the air filling her body again at such a pace made her feel lightheaded.

"It's okay, Emily. Take it easy. Come back to me."

Come back to me. It had been a long time since someone had said that. Wait, who was with me?

Blinking in the darkness, Emily looked up at the hulking shape boave her. One with a sleek, muscular chest bare and glistening with sweat, light from the hallway casting his hair in a silvery sheen.

Mike.

Then Emily came back to reality. Mike was here. In her apartment. Shirtless. Sitting on her bed leaning over her as he stroked her forehead.

That is a sight I could certainly get used to.

Shut up.

"Emily?" Mike frowned at her. "Are you okay now?"

Emily's mind had gone momentarily blank. She was getting distracted by how nice it felt to be stroked like this. The last person who had done it was her mother when she was ten. Emily found herself wanting to purr and curl into him, asking for more. Swallowing hard, Emily managed to find her voice.

"What...what happened?"

"You were having a nightmare. Your screams woke me up." Mike shrugged. "I didn't know what the hell was going on. I thought you were being attacked."

"I was." Emily's voice broke. "I was remembering...that night when..."

She couldn't say it. Even now, it was still too much for her to handle. Emily closed her eyes and looked away. She would not cry, not in front of Mike. Mike's hand stilled, but he didn't pull away. There was silence, Emily stiffening as she realized Mike wasn't leaving. She didn't want him to go, but she didn't want him to see her like this. So weak and helpless.

Then Mike shifted on the bed, his hand leaving her forehead and then he was carefully lifting her upright. Emily was too stunned to fight back and gasped as Mike made her lean into him, resting her head on his shoulder as his arms wrapped around her.

"It's okay. I've got you." His voice was so soft, so gentle. "Cry if you want."

Emily was too surprised to cry. Mike's reaction was not what she had expected. Then she found herself sinking into his arms as she hugged him back. He smelled really good, and that chest of his was solid and warm. Very warm. Emily could feel his heartbeat against her chest, a steady, soothing pace. Mike stroked her hair, shifting himself a little but he never lowered his arms. He simply held her.

When was the last time someone had held her like this? Certainly not Darryl. He wasn't much of a cuddler once the novelty of their relationship had worn off. Pretty much the only time he cuddled was when he wanted something sexual. There was nothing sexual in Mike's hold. Not really.

They stayed like that for a while, Emily reluctant to pull away. She felt warm and protected for the first time since her attack. Marsden had taken a lot from her, and Emily had been desperately trying to claw it back. Just a simple hug from a man and already Emily found herself calming. It felt good. Really good.

"You okay now?" Mike whispered. His hand was still stroking her hair. "Feeling better."

"A bit." Emily bit her lip. "I don't like being like this. It's not me."

"I know. Nobody likes it." Mike's arms tightened around her. "What happened, Emily? Can you talk about it?"

"I...I want to but..." Emily drew back a little and looked up. Mike's face was inches from hers. Far too close for comfort. Her pulse spiked as she found herself staring at his mouth. "I can't say anymore until my boss says you've been cleared."

"I see."

From his tone, Mike did see, but he didn't like it.

He still didn't move away. Emily was finding it harder to breathe, and it was nothing to do with her dream. This time her heart was racing. Just the closeness from this man was sending her into near overdrive. Emily wanted to reach out and see if he tasted as good as she imagined.

She licked her lips, and Mike's eyes snagged on her mouth. His eyes seemed to darken, and his nostrils flared. Emily felt a shiver down her back. God, he was enticing. If she leaned forward a little, would he...

Mike released her slowly and eased back. Then he rose to his feet, clearing his throat.

"Get some sleep." He said gruffly. "I'll see you in the morning. And no more nightmares."

Then he was practically running from the room, closing the door behind him. Emily was left bewildered. What had just happened there? One moment, she was sure Mike was going to kiss her, and then the next moment he was gone. Had she done something wrong?

Emily was sure that Mike had been about to kiss her. When he left the room just now, Emily saw the large bulge in his jeans, too big to hide. He was aroused, very so.

So why hadn't he done anything about it?

When sleep did come to her tonight, Emily was sure she was going to be having a dream that was going to leave her wanting.

Chapter Ten

He was an idiot. A big idiot. Mike scowled at the ceiling as he settled down on Emily's couch. It wasn't really long enough for him to lie down comfortably. He had slept on worse things in the army, but this felt like torture.

Especially when there was a perfectly good bed close by with a beautiful woman in it.

He had been about to kiss her. Emily was in his arms and he had wanted to press her into the bed and taste that lovely mouth. But then Mike had stood up and practically sprinted out of the room.

He had to be mad. What man in their right mind would walk away from someone like Emily? Especially after lusting about her for months.

This whole day had turned into a crazy mess. Mike didn't even know where to start with it. He thought the murder was bad enough. But to know that Emily wasn't who she claimed and that she might be involved? That was just hard to swallow.

Mike was tempted to go back, see if Emily was still awake. But he stopped himself. She had just been attacked and that nightmare had frightened her, never mind him. The last thing she needed was to be jumped on by her boss.

Although from the look in her eyes before he almost kissed her, she would have willingly accepted it.

Mike swiped it all out of his head - and failed - and tried to get some sleep. There were a lot of answers he wanted and he wasn't going anywhere until he got them. Emily had promised that, at least. Now he just had to wait.

And the wait was agonizing. Especially when he knew for sure that Emily wanted him.

God, he was such a fool. Maybe he had been single for too long if someone as young as Emily was becoming desirable. Mike wouldn't have been surprised if Emily had slapped him and told him to get lost. But she hadn't. And she had felt really good in his arms.

Enough of that. You need answers. Then decide if there's anything there.

Oh, there's going to be something there. I know it.

Somehow, Mike managed to close his eyes and get some sleep. It wasn't much, and the angle he lay on the couch was uncomfortable with the erection he had sporting, but he managed. He had the temptation to ease the pressure in his cock, but he didn't think that would take the edge off. It was only going to ease once it got what it wanted.

Emily.

When Mike woke up, it was daylight. The curtains were open and light was cast across the couch right in his face. Blinking in the bright light, Mike eased himself up to sitting. His head was pounding, and his arousal was at a dull ache. It was going to be a task to walk around knowing that the woman he desired was close by and he wasn't able to touch her as he wanted.

Not yet. But soon.

There was the sound of someone in the kitchen. Someone moving around and the sound of a kettle boiling. Emily was already awake. Mike had heard her complain that she wasn't an early riser, so he was expecting her to have gone back to bed.

Getting to his feet, Mike grabbed at his shirt and put it on. It felt better having a barrier between him and Emily. It had been dark in her room, but he had seen hunger flare in her eyes when she saw that he wasn't wearing a shirt. Mike shivered at the thought of having Emily touch him again.

Stop it!

Mike entered the kitchen. Emily was at the hob with a frying pan. Something was sizzling in it, and the delicious aromas wafted past Mike's nose. His stomach growled, and then his cock flared back to life when he took in Emily. The back view was even better than the front. She wore pale pink running shorts that hugged her thighs and backside and a black racer-back top. She was barefoot and slick with sweat, her clothes sticking to her. Her hair was up in a high ponytail, her ponytail swaying as she moved.

Had she been out on a run? Mike hadn't heard her leave or come back. Showed how good he was keeping an eye on her.

Emily suddenly tensed. Then she looked over her shoulder, and Mike saw her eyes darken when she took him in.

"Oh. Hey."

"Hey." Mike shoved his hands in his pockets and leaned on the doorframe. "You been out already?"

"I needed to go for a run. Get rid of some excess energy." Emily waved the spatula at him. "And don't worry that I could've been hurt. I was very much aware of people around me. No one followed me or took a pot shot."

"You still went out on your own."

Emily rolled her eyes.

"I'm not defenceless, Mike. I can take care of myself."

"I don't doubt that." Mike drawled. "But defenceless does often equate to stupidity."

Emily glared at him. She growled and turned away. Good. Better to have her pissed off at him than looking at him like she wanted to have him for breakfast instead. She kept her back to him as she took the pan off the hob and began to heap the food onto two plates.

"Am I going into work today?"

"You can if you want to, but after what happened last night, I would advise against it."

"Are you giving me permission to be off work?"

Mike grinned.

"Definitely."

Emily grunted, still not looking at him. She picked up the plates and put them on the kitchen table. Then she waved a hand in the direction of the kettle.

"If you want coffee, help yourself. Everything's there."

"Thanks."

Mike watched her as Emily filled a glass of water and then sat down. She kept her eyes averted, her jaw tense but with a deep red flush across her cheeks. He couldn't make up her mind if she was angry or fighting back arousal. Mike guessed Emily wasn't completely sure, either.

Mike went to the counter, fighting back a wince as his knee screamed at him. Lying as he had all night, his injury hadn't been too impressed. It was now at a level where he couldn't ignore the pain. He gritted his teeth as he fixed himself a coffee, but he couldn't stop himself from limping as he came back to the table. Emily looked up and frowned.

"You okay?"

"I'm fine." Mike eased himself into the chair gingerly, wincing as his knee and thigh made the pain build. He was going to be rolling around on the floor soon. "Have you got any painkillers?"

"Of course."

Emily stood and hurried to a door by the sink. Moments later, a box of painkillers was put by Mike's coffee cup. Emily stood over him, her expression now one of concern.

"Are you sure you're okay? You went a bit white just now."

"It's nothing unusual." Mike reached for the box and opened it, cracking out two painkillers from the pack. "It's just my knee. Sleeping as I did hasn't done it any good."

Emily now looked pained herself.

"You should've told me. I could've let you sleep with me. I mean…" Her face went bright red. "It's big enough for two, and it's comfortable enough."

"I wasn't about to intrude." Although the thought of being in bed with Emily was enticing. Mike growled and took the pills, washing them down with the coffee that burned his mouth. "I'm used to sleeping alone, so you might've ended up on the floor."

"I was going to say the same." Emily hesitated. Then she hurried back to her chair. "How did you get hurt? I don't think I've ever asked."

"Afghanistan." Mike looked at the food before him. A cooked breakfast. He hadn't had one of those in a while. It looked a little burnt and haphazardly placed on the plate, but nothing had looked more delicious. He picked up his fork and speared a piece of bacon. "I was near an IED mine when it went off.

I was lucky not to lose my leg, but my knee was shot to pieces. They had to put a rod in my leg to match my fibula and a metal plate to replace my knee." And years later, Mike could still feel it. "Part of my femur has been replaced as well."

Emily stared at him, her eyes wide.

"Jesus. I've been overseas, but I've never been in that situation. I just deal with crooked soldiers, make sure they keep in line."

"And that is a job I wouldn't touch with a barge pole." Mike said. "You get seen as a snitch. Squaddies are supposed to stick together, not rat each other out."

"Someone's gotta do it. And being a soldier is dangerous. You want to know someone's there to cover you and not put your life on the line."

Fair point. Mike wasn't comfortable around the MPs in the army, but he appreciated the work they had to do. Someone had to make sure soldiers looked after each other and didn't betray them by dealing with the enemy or stealing contraband. There had been times when Mike had seen betrayal happen when they were most needed to protect, and the MPs had swooped in. They were ruthless people.

Emily didn't look ruthless. But he had never seen her at work.

Did she look as good in her uniform?

"What made you want to become a soldier?"

Emily blinked. She hadn't expected that. Licking her lips, she went back to spearing the sausage she had cut up.

"My stepdad and my brother are in the armed forces. My grandfathers on both sides were in Vietnam and the Korean War."

"Runs in the family, then."

"You could say that." Emily sighed. "It's shocking to know there are so many bad squaddies out there. When there are a few bad apples in the barrel, several others are bound to get bruised."

That was the most appropriate description of the situation Mike had ever heard. Emily did a tough job, even tougher than what he had done. He certainly couldn't investigate other soldiers and arrest them. It felt like he was betraying his own people. But Emily managed it. She was certainly tougher than he was.

He had a newfound respect for her. Emily did a job not many people would take on, and from the way she talked about it as they ate, she was passionate. You didn't get passion like that nowadays.

But she purposefully kept away from why she was in Union in the first place. Mike was itching to ask and why she had woken up screaming in the night. It had to be connected to what had happened to her. But he couldn't. Emily wouldn't tell him.

Not until her boss was sure he was safe to tell. Mike didn't like being put under a microscope, but he understood. And he wanted to be there. He wanted to help. Anything to help Emily.

Come off it. You're only doing this because you're desperate for her to stay in Union. It's doubtful she's going to stay much longer if her cover is blown.

I'll make her stay.

Mike was almost finished with his food - a little greasy and a little burnt, but it went down well - when there was a knock at the door. Mike tensed, wishing he hadn't left his gun in the living room. But Emily held up a hand.

"Ease down, Mike. That'll be my boss. He said he would be here about this time."

That still didn't make Mike feel any better. Because now he had to face Emily's commanding officer. And that had a knot building in his stomach.

#

Emily hurried to the door, trying not to look back at Mike still sitting at her table. He looked very much at home there, and that had lots of emotions swirling around in Emily's gut. Emotions that shouldn't have any place there.

Why couldn't she have an unattractive boss? This would be so much easier.

Taking a deep breath, Emily opened the door. A tall, slim man in his late fifties with snow-white hair and a broad face stood in the hallway. It took a moment for Emily to realize this was her commanding officer. She had never seen him in anything other than a uniform. Now he wore black slacks and a white shirt open at the neck, coupled with a black leather jacket.

Kenneth Chambers' expression didn't change, but his eyes softened when he saw her. Then he stepped into her apartment, surprising Emily even more by giving her a brief hug.

"You okay?"

"Just about." Emily swayed as he released her. "Mike Wilson is still here."

"He stayed all night?"

"On the couch." Emily shook her head when Chambers raised his eyebrows. "Don't, Sir. I've got a splitting headache. Let's just get this done."

Chambers grunted. Then he turned towards the kitchen. Mike was filling the doorway, his arms folded as he leaned on the doorframe. Emily could see that he was keeping weight off his bad knee. Mike fixed Chambers with a hard stare, one that was matched with one from Chambers. Emily groaned and closed the door.

"Don't start, please, Mike. I'm not in the mood." She gestured at her boss. "This is my commanding officer, Colonel Kenneth Chambers. Mike Wilson."

"Sergeant Mike Wilson." Mike straightened up and saluted. "Sir."

Of course. It was at times like this that Emily forgot Mike had been in the army himself. She cleared her throat and gestured towards the living room.

"Let's go in there. I think we all need to sit down."

Chambers grunted. He followed her in. Mike joined them a moment later, his limp more prominent. Emily felt a pang of sympathy for him. It had to hurt walking around after having most of your leg shattered the way Mike's had. She certainly wouldn't be able to cope.

Mike eased himself with a relieved sigh into an armchair, stretching his bad leg out. Chambers sat on the couch, still scowling at Mike.

"Don't think I'm happy about this, Wilson. Emily shouldn't have got you involved in this."

"She got me involved the moment your people got me to hire her. Besides," Mike shrugged as he folded his arms, "I'm a nosy bugger."

Chambers grunted.

"No argument there." He looked up at Emily. "He's come up clean."

"Nice to know you trust me." Mike grumbled.

"We have to make sure you're not going to tell the people after Emily where she is."

"They already know where she is."

Emily groaned and held up her hands.

"Whoa, enough. Mike is a good guy, Sir. I trust him, and that's enough for me."

The look she got from Mike was one of stunned amazement. Then the surprise cleared and his expression warmed, giving her a brief nod. Chambers grunted.

"Okay, fine. Just tell him. I'm sure a man of his calibre isn't going to walk away now."

Emily knew that for certain. She found herself pacing around the room. She should sit, but now she was restless. Taking a few deep breaths, Emily turned to Mike.

"There was a squaddie who worked as an MP on my team. Sergeant Eddie Marsden. He was known for being a bully with the lower ranks. Good at his job, although some of his methods were questionable. But he got results. His private life, however, was not good at all. He went through a string of girlfriends while I was working with him. They never lasted long."

"Why's that?" Mike's eyes narrowed. "Was he abusive?"

"Yes. His girlfriends would often turn up to see him with a black eye or a split lip. One girl had her arm in a cast. Claimed she hurt herself falling down the stairs." Emily saw Mike's jaw clench. "But none of them would say that Marsden had hurt them. They just got out of there as soon as they could and Marsden moved on to the next victim. And then his last girlfriend decided to take a stand."

Susan Grey had had no qualms about calling the MPs on Marsden after he hit her, barely weeks into their relationship. She was a nurse and an advocate for domestic violence, and she wouldn't stand for it. Emily had to admire that about her. Susan was stronger than most women, including her.

Emily resumed her pacing.

"When we raided his place to arrest Marsden, we found a huge supply of weapons and drugs in the basement." She rubbed her stomach as it churned. She could still remember going down there and finding the containment. "Going through his computer records, we discovered he was selling them on the black market. The mafia, militia, even our enemies in Syria and

Afghanistan were customers. Anything to the highest bidder and Marsden was making a lot of money out of it."

Mike let out a hiss in a muffled curse. Chambers' expression didn't change. He simply sat there grimly, watching Mike. Emily rubbed her hands on her thighs. Her palms were getting sweaty as she remembered the aftermath.

"I was the one who arrested him. Read him his rights. Marsden and I have never gotten along, and he hated the fact that a woman had arrested him. He vowed that he would get his own back, that he wouldn't let me get one over on him." Emily shuddered. "No woman got the better of him."

She was looking at the floor, unable to look at either of the two men with her. There was a rustling of clothes and then footsteps. Bare feet appeared, and then Emily felt her chin being lifted in a gentle touch. She looked up and found herself looking at Mike. He gave her a gentle smile as he brushed a thumb across her jaw. It was then Emily realized she was shaking and Mike's touch was calming her.

"What happened?" He pressed.

Emily licked her lips. She knew her boss was watching them, but she couldn't bring herself to pull back.

"The trial happened. Everyone had testified and it was about to be wrapped up. The night before he was due to be sentenced, he broke out of jail and went after me."

Mike's hand stilled. Something close to understanding burned in his eyes.

"He tried to kill you. In your home."

Now he knew why she had freaked out during the night. Emily swallowed. Even now, her throat hurt with the memory.

"Yes. I lived off the barracks, and he got in while I was asleep. He…" Emily put her hands to her throat. "He tried to strangle me. I couldn't breathe. I…"

"Hey, it's okay." Mike wrapped his arms around her, tucking her head under his chin. "He's not here now. You're okay."

Emily wasn't sure about that, but she was glad that Mike was holding her. It felt good. Really good. When was the last time someone had held her like this, made her feel better? Emily couldn't remember. Darryl hadn't been able to do that towards the end.

But Darryl wasn't Mike.

Emily wanted to wrap her arms around Mike and sink into his embrace, but she was very aware of Chambers watching them with a scowl. Did he suspect that there was something going on between the two of them? Emily eased away from Mike, stepping back so she didn't have the urge to touch him.

"Marsden had tripped a silent alarm, which is connected to my team on the base. They were there and got to me in time. Marsden had disappeared and went on the run, and I had to spend the night in hospital." Emily brushed her fingers over her neck. "Colonel Chambers was concerned that Marsden could try it again, especially as he had threatened me in front of witnesses. Then I was shot at outside my parents' house a few days later. He didn't want to take the chance that Marsden could try again, or get someone to do it for him."

"So he put you in witness protection." Mike murmured.

"Sort of." Chambers grunted. "This isn't sanctioned by the US Marshals, but by my office. Emily's currently in hiding with our expenses until Marsden's been dealt with."

Mike turned to Chambers.

"Have you not found Marsden?"

"Marsden's gone to ground. We haven't been able to get anything on him." Chambers shook his head. "I don't like it, but until he's found and put in maximum security, Emily's life is being threatened."

Everything on hold. Living more of a lie until the man who tried to kill her was apprehended. Emily had done undercover before, but this was something else. She hated it. But now someone else in her new life knew about it, and that made her feel like she had some sort of ally. Now Emily didn't feel as suffocated as before. She could breathe a little better.

Although breathing properly around Mike Wilson was not always easy.

"Now her cover's been blown." Chambers rose to his feet. "She needs to go into a safe house."

Mike frowned.

"Why a safe house? I'm not going to tell anyone."

"You may not, but Marsden had clearly found Emily. And God only knows how many people are helping him. Telling you about this was to stop you from getting Emily into further danger, but that's it."

"Instead, you've put me in danger as well." Mike snapped. "Marsden finds out that I know, he's going to target me."

"Which is why we need to move Emily now before that happens." Chambers turned to Emily. "Get your things packed, Emily. We'll be leaving in an hour. I've already got a place set up for you."

Moving again? Emily had only just gotten used to the life she had been given. She hated the name Molly, and she hated being a waitress, but to uproot herself all over again? Emily shook her head.

"I'm not going anywhere."

Chambers groaned.

"O'Rourke…"

"Don't start with me, Colonel." Emily snapped. "I'm not packing up and moving every time my cover is blown, otherwise I'm going to be on the run forever. It's not going to work. How are you supposed to capture Marsden when I'm constantly moving around?"

Chambers blinked. Then he frowned.

"Are you saying that you're staying here? You do realize that now he knows where you are, you're going to be a sitting duck."

"You want Marsden? I can get him." Emily lifted her chin defiantly. "I can get him to come to me. He wants me? He can come and get me."

Chambers stared. So did Mike.

"You're putting yourself up as bait?" Mike sounded dazed. "He's going to kill you when he catches up to you."

Emily rolled her eyes.

"You two keep forgetting that I'm not just a woman. I'm a soldier first, and I know the stakes here. But I'm not going to go on the run forever." She turned to Chambers. "You let me do my goddamn job, Sir. I'm not good to you running around with a ghost chasing my tail. If you can't do that, too bad."

If Chambers couldn't let her do her job, Emily would just do it herself without his consent. She was tired of running. Marsden had got her jumping at shadows and Emily hated that she couldn't completely trust anyone now.

Not entirely true. She trusted Mike. There was no doubt about that. But that wouldn't be enough. Emily couldn't go into hiding again. Marsden had taken too much of the past year already. He wasn't about to take anymore.

Chambers scowled. He didn't look happy at all. *Too bad, I'm not changing my mind.* Finally, her boss sighed and looked away, still scowling.

"Okay, fine. But you can't stay here. From what you've said, Marsden knows where you are, and it's not as protected as I thought. You need to be somewhere that's going to be a bit more of a protection for you, and you don't leave that place."

"I'm not going to a safe house!"

"Then what do you suggest?"

"She comes with me."

Emily and Chambers spun around. Mike watched both of them with a blank stare. Emily wasn't quite sure she had heard him properly. Chambers looked equally startled.

"You what?"

"I've got a secure home. And I'm licensed to carry." Mike looked at Emily. "She stays with me. Then she's got a safe place to stay and someone to make sure she doesn't get into trouble."

Chambers spluttered.

"But...that...she can't go there!"

"Why not?"

Chambers tried to find a reason. But Emily had already made up her mind. It was probably a bad idea, given the tension between them, but it was either that or go into that damn safe house.

"I'll do it."

Chambers stared at her like she had gone mad. Maybe she had. But Emily knew her options were limited. This seemed like the best option, better than living in an apartment where the walls were closing in on her.

Although she might regret it with Mike in such close quarters day and night.

Chapter Eleven

M ike knew he had taken leave of his senses by saying that he would have Emily at his home, but his instincts had kicked in. He didn't want her going anywhere. If Chambers moved her now, Emily could disappear again. She may fight it, but she would leave. And Mike didn't want her leaving.

Where better to keep her close than at his home?

Chambers was clearly not happy about this, and he stood in the corner scowling as Emily packed a few things. He and Emily had gone into her bedroom and argued in loud whispers for a good ten minutes. Mike didn't intrude, but he could figure out what was being said. Emily refused to be moved as Chambers wanted, and Chambers didn't believe having Emily at Mike's home was the best option.

In any normal situation, Mike would agree. But this wasn't a normal situation. And this was Emily involved. Mike wouldn't be walking away anytime soon.

Damn, you're such a goner.

Within half an hour, Emily had her things in the back of Mike's car and she was locking up. She walked away from it without a backward glance. Mike felt a pinch of pain around his chest at the sight. The apartment had merely been a place to put her head down and a moment of respite. It wasn't her home. She didn't have a home right now.

And if this wasn't resolved, the chances of going back to her old life were diminishing. Mike had never been in that position before, but he couldn't imagine how tough it was to detach yourself from everything.

Chambers waited by Emily's car as Mike and Emily put her things in the back. He fixed Mike with a hard glare.

"Make sure she doesn't do anything stupid. Same goes to you."

"And what sort of stupidity do you think I'm going to get up to?"

The two men glared at each other. Chambers broke first, rolling his eyes as he turned to Emily.

"Are you sure about this?"

"I'm sure." Emily didn't blink as she responded. "He's made me run once already. I'm not running again. And Mike's going to look after me. I'll be protected."

Protected. Mike felt his chest tighten. He would be doing more than protect Emily. Marsden was not going to get his hands on her. Not if he had anything to do it with.

Leaving Chambers behind to secure the flat, Mike drove them away from the apartment. He caught Emily watching the place she had called home for almost a year disappear in the wing mirror, but she didn't say anything. There wasn't really much he could say. Emily was probably going through a myriad of emotions right now. He wouldn't be able to touch on just one of them.

Mike wanted to reach out and take her hand, squeeze her thigh, anything to give her some comfort. But he kept his hands on the wheel. He needed to keep himself restrained. Not a good idea to touch her right now. The tension between them had been building all morning, and Mike could feel it pressing down on him. He made a move, it would explode.

Now is not the time to be thinking about Emily like she's your woman.

That's the problem. She's been my woman since she walked into the restaurant. I'm only just beginning to realize it.

They drove on in silence and into the suburbs where Mike and Prudence lived. Where he was, it was secluded enough that the neighbors weren't going to be nosy, and with the alarms Mike had set up around his land, they would be armed and ready before anyone got to the house. Prudence had called it extreme, teasing him about still being in the army, but Mike felt better knowing that his home was protected.

Emily would be protected here. Once he set a few traps around the edge of his land. That would make Mike feel slightly better. Providing Emily didn't leave the premises, she was safe. He could keep her safe.

Mike had encountered dangerous soldiers in his time serving. Most of them had been on his side and they were the scarier ones. To have a former teammate break into her home and try to kill her had to be tough to handle. Mike didn't think he would be able to cope with it, either. Maybe not as well as Emily; she was doing really well considering the circumstances. It was hard not to feel some admiration for her.

Emily O'Rourke was full of surprises.

They turned into Mike's driveway and pulled into the carport. Mike got out, stretching his legs with a grimace. Even with the seat pushed back, his knees were killing him from being cramped in the small car. He would be glad to get his jeep back.

If his friend could put it back together.

"This is your place?"

Mike turned. Emily had got out of the car and was staring at his house with something close to wonder.

"Sure is. Anything wrong?"

"Erm, no, of course not." Emily cleared her throat, not able to look him in the eye. "It's not what I was expecting, I guess. I just...I don't know."

Mike laughed. That just made Emily go bright red. He opened up the trunk.

"My wife and I picked this place out because it was in a neighborhood but we didn't have neighbors looking over our fence. We could be part of a community and have our own space at the same time." He picked out Emily's laptop bag and held it out. "Now it's just me and a teenager taking up the space. And there are times when my daughter is taking up more space than I am."

"I can imagine." Emily's mouth twitched as she took her bag, careful not to touch him. "Prudence has a tendency to leave things all over the restaurant when she comes to see you. I can't begin to imagine what your office looks like."

"Like I've been thrown into a brightly colored thrift store if I don't bring it home with me." Taking out the other two backpacks, Mike shut the trunk and locked it. "Let's go on in."

He led the way up the path to the front door. As he opened up, Mike was very aware of Emily close behind him. He could feel the heat from her body pressing up against his back. His body stirred to life again, and Mike bit back a growl. Now was not the time. He needed to get Emily settled and then he was going to check the property. Then Mike could relax, just a little.

Why did he say that he would do this? Because even with Emily close and knowing she was safe wasn't going to make Mike relax. He now had temptation under his nose. Emily was not here to be pawed and groped by an old man.

Emily doesn't see you as old. She sees you as a man she wants.

That just makes it worse.

Mike heard a voice in the living room, and he sighed. Prudence was home. Normally on a Saturday, she headed out to see friends. Signalling at Emily to put her things in the hall, Mike headed into the lounge. Prudence was sitting in an armchair with her laptop over on her lap, her cell phone pressed to her ear.

"Oh, hi, Dad."

"Hey, honey. Is Colette around?"

"No, she's already gone home. I'm meeting her later with some friends."

"Good." Mike gestured towards the door. "Would you mind ending the call? I've got someone here."

"Sure." Prudence ended the call with a quick goodbye and sat up, putting her laptop aside. "Do you want me to go to my room and leave you to it?"

"No, you're fine. But I do need you to help Emily settle in while I go and check a few things."

Prudence frowned.

"Emily? Who's Emily?"

Oh, yes. Mike had gotten used to calling Emily by her real name over a few hours that he had forgotten that Emily was known by another name. Chambers wasn't going to be impressed at this, but Prudence was his kid.

89

Mike knew she could be discreet.

"Emily is…well…" Mike looked over his shoulder. "You've met Prudence, haven't you?"

"I have." Emily moved into the doorway and gave Prudence a half-smile. "Hey, kid."

Prudence's eyes widened. She shot to her feet.

"Molly? You're Emily?"

"Yep." Emily glanced at Mike. "This is a long story and it…it's complicated. The less you know about it the better."

"I see." Prudence put her hands on her hips and frowned at her father. "Why does everyone treat me like I'm a child, Dad?"

"Because you are in my eyes." Mike shot back. "And Emily's right. The less you know the better. Telling you her real name is as far as we're willing to do it."

Prudence looked from Mike to Emily and back again. Her confusion was going, and now she was beginning to look worried.

"Dad, what's happening? You're not in trouble, are you?"

"No, of course not." Mike took a deep breath. "But Emily is. As long as we keep this between us, it shouldn't go any further. Emily's just going to stay for a couple of days until things get sorted out."

Prudence stared at him a moment longer. Then she smiled and nodded.

"Sure, Dad. At least I've got someone to talk to who might have an inkling of what I'm talking about."

"You make me sound like I'm a dinosaur."

"I'm pleading the fifth on that." Prudence stepped around her father, squeezing his arm as she passed. "Come on, Emily. I'll show you to the guest room. Then I'll give you a little tour."

"Thanks." Emily turned to Mike. "What are you going to do?"

"I'm going to check the area, make sure things are secure." Mike swallowed. "I'll be back soon."

Emily nodded, her eyes drifting over his face. She looked like she was going to say something, but decided against it. Then she turned and disappeared into the hall. It was only then that Mike could breathe properly.

Hopefully, a tour of the perimeter in the intense heat would help squash his need to follow Emily into that guest room. Mike needed to get his head on straight before he went any further with this.

But further with what? Helping Emily find a dangerous soldier, or getting her into his bed?

#

Prudence kept talking as she led Emily upstairs and showed her into the guest room at the far end of the hall. Emily let her; it was nice to hear something that wasn't to do with her mess right now. Listening to random things from an eighteen-year-old felt like a breath of fresh air.

Emily liked Prudence. She was bouncy, a little too much for her father, but she was personable and there was always a smile. Until someone pissed her off and then Emily saw a side of Prudence that was coldly controlled and made her seem to grow several inches. She was Mike's daughter, no doubt about it.

Maybe having Prudence around would be a good thing. Emily was intensely aware of the tension between her and Mike, and it was going to brew over soon if they were going to be in close quarters for a long period of time. When they were at work, Emily was always on the go so she didn't have time to think too much about how hot her boss was. And she had the chance to get away at the end of the day.

Now she had no opportunity to do that. Chambers had reluctantly agreed to Emily going to Mike's house but she was not to leave the grounds. She had to stay in the house. Emily was going to go stir crazy, both by staring at four walls and by knowing the man she lusted after was close by and she wasn't able to do anything to release the tension.

Perhaps she should have thought this through a bit more first.

Prudence left Emily with her bags, saying that she would be downstairs if Emily needed anything and giving her a couple of towels. She winked at Emily, saying that a shower might be in order. Emily couldn't agree more. She had gone for a run before dawn after struggling to sleep, and she didn't think it was appropriate to shower with her boss and Mike so close by. Not that she would have had any time to do it considering how fast they got out of her apartment.

The guest room had a separate bathroom with a decent-sized shower and bathtub. The bath looked very tempting; Emily's apartment had only had a shower. She hadn't had a bath since before she left her home.

Emily gave in. She ran a bath, putting in a lot of bubble bath. Then she stripped down and slid into the hot water with a sigh. This felt like heaven. Emily had loved a bath when she was back at home, especially after a long day at work. It had the ability to ease everything away and calm her mind. Emily's mind never stopped going, not even in sleep. Just when she was soaking in the bath.

Things were still racing around in her head, but it eased the longer she stayed in the bath. Emily closed her eyes and allowed herself a few moments to relax. She needed this. If she could have a good soak, it might soothe her enough to sleep properly. After her nightmare and Mike leaving her in a state of confusion, Emily had struggled to settle again. Maybe she would after this.

Then she would get on with finding Marsden. He had been elusive so far, but Emily hadn't been actively searching for him. She would be able to find him, and Marsden knew it. Coming after her had been a mistake. Now Emily was out for blood.

The bath did the trick. Emily managed to get out of the bath, bright red and wrinkled, and dried off before she fell naked into bed. The mattress was soft, the sheets clean and the duvet nice and thick. Normally, Emily slept with some clothes on, but she was too tired to root around in her backs. She simply curled up and closed her eyes.

When she opened them again, the room was still light, but she could see the sun through the window and it was lower in the sky. It had to be late in the afternoon. She had slept for at least eight hours. Emily didn't normally sleep through the day, but that showed how much she needed it. She was feeling better for it as well.

Slipping out of bed, Emily dressed in jeans and a loose jumper that had once belonged to her brother. It went down to her knees and Emily had to roll up the sleeves, but it felt good to have something of her family with her. Emily buried her nose into the jumper and took a deep breath. It still smelled like Nate.

Would she be able to contact them now? Emily hadn't been able to speak to her family for a long time, only briefly before she was put on a plane. They knew the situation and they understood, but none of them liked it. Her brother, especially, was furious that he couldn't be told as a fellow squaddie. But Emily had pleaded with him to leave it be. If he knew more than he did, Marsden could use that against him. He had shown that he was not above going after Emily. What was to stop him going after her family?

He had gotten to Karen. And Samir. Marsden knew where she was, and that meant the net was going to squeeze tighter around her. Emily planned to make sure she had a weapon to get herself out of it.

It was quiet as Emily went downstairs. No voices, and the TV wasn't on. Prudence wasn't anywhere to be seen, but there was noise coming from the kitchen. The sound of the radio playing classical music.

Emily entered the kitchen, and stopped short. Mike was at the counter chopping vegetables. The radio was on near his elbow and he seemed to be humming along to it. Emily had never heard Mike sing, never mind hum. He wasn't completely tuneless. He did need a few lessons, but he could keep to the rhythm. He had that going for him.

Classical music was not what Emily had expected of her boss. Then again, there was a lot about him she hadn't expected.

"Hey."

Mike stopped chopping and looked around. He smiled, and it made his eyes twinkle.

"Hey. I take it you slept well."

"Very. I think I needed it." Emily looked at the clock and winced. "Shit. I've been asleep for ten hours."

"Like you said, you needed it. I left you alone so you could rest." Mike flushed and looked away. "I had...other things to do, anyway."

"I remembered." Emily sat down at the kitchen table. "Did you sort out the perimeter?"

"Yes. Everything's sorted. If Marsden tries to sneak in, he's going to get caught." Mike glanced at her as he resumed chopping. "He's not getting anywhere near you."

Emily partially wished he would. She was spoiling for a fight more than anything. Marsden had taken a lot from her, and she was hiding like a coward. He wasn't going to take anymore of that from her.

"Where's Prudence?"

"She's gone to see a few friends. Studying for exams on Monday, she calls it."

"You don't believe her."

Mike smiled.

"I'm a father and I was once eighteen myself. Prudence does study, but she's not very good at doing it with other people. She can get...distracted."

Emily laughed.

"Sounds like a teenager, all right. But aren't you concerned about her?"

"She's eighteen, and I made sure she had a license to carry. That girl can shoot the bullseye out of a target." Mike picked up the chopping board and slid the vegetables into a frying pan, the oil making everything sizzle. "She'll be fine. If I put her in a gilded cage, she's going to find a way to get out."

"What does that say about what you're doing with me?"

Mike's smile faded. He stared at her.

"Looking out for a friend. And after seeing Karen Underwood's body, I'm not taking any chances."

Emily had no response for that. She sat at the table and watched as Mike moved around the kitchen, chopping more vegetables and then adding diced chicken to the pan and stirring it. Emily couldn't stop herself from watching his hands as he went on with his cooking. He really was good with his hands.

I wonder what his hands would be like on my body.

Enough. You'll be here with his daughter as well. That should be enough to cool you down.

That was the problem. It didn't cool anything down.

As everything cooked in the pan, Mike picked out some pitta bread from the bread bin, tearing them in half and putting them on plates he had set out. Once the chicken was cooked, he then started to fill up the pitta pockets. The smell of the food reached Emily's nostrils and her stomach growled. Mike chuckled.

"Hungry, are you?"

"Do you need to ask?"

"Well, this should help for a bit." Mike brought the two plates to the table and placed one in front of her before going to the fridge and retrieving two soda cans. "I'm not a chef, but it should do for now."

"Anything will do right now." Emily grimaced. "It can't be any worse than my food this morning. I'm not much of a cook."

"It was edible, and that's enough for me." Mike winked. "I'm not fussy when it comes to food as long as it's now raw."

"Not a sushi man, then."

"Not a chance. I prefer things when they're dead and filleted." Mike reached for his can and opened it. "I don't want my dinner waving at me first."

Emily giggled. She picked up one of the pitta pockets and took a bite. She couldn't stop herself from moaning.

"This is really good."

"You sound surprised again."

"Oh." Emily shrugged. "I guess I'm getting a lot of surprises today."

Especially from Mike. He had offered her a place to stay now hers was compromised, he lived in one of those houses that anyone would be jealous of, and he could cook. What else could he do?

If you hang in there, maybe you'll find out.

And Emily wanted to find out.

Chapter Twelve

It wasn't long before Emily had wolfed down the rest of her food. They didn't speak, the silence comfortable as Emily concentrated on eating. She glugged down her soda a little too fast, munching away on the mish-mash of food Mike had put together. It did taste damn good. She could happily eat this every day.

It beat cooking herself and then her food coming out charred.

Emily felt a belch coming. Too many bubbles. She covered her hand with her mouth and managed to stifle it. Across the table, Mike was fighting back a laugh as he reached for his own can. Emily groaned.

"God, sorry about that."

"Least you were polite about it." Mike's eyes twinkled. "Prudence just lets them out and no apology."

"She is a teenager, so no surprise." Emily lowered his hand. She could still feel the bubbles in her throat. "My parents raised me better. That doesn't mean...I mean..."

God, she had to be as red as her hair. Why did she have to put her foot in it?

"No offence taken." Mike winked. "I like to think Prudence isn't my kid at times. Just so I can complain about the parenting."

Emily laughed. She sat back in her chair, rubbing her belly.

"That was really good, Mike. I think I needed that more than I realized." She sighed. "I feel like I don't deserve any of this."

"Hey, we're squaddies. I may not be enlisted anymore but I can still look out for you."

"I'm glad." More than he knew. Emily fought back a yawn. "It's why Chambers thought you would be a good boss for me. Ex-soldiers are reliable and he knew I would be in good hands."

In good hands. Why did she have to say that? Why didn't she just get up and leave before she put her foot in it again and started to sink?

Mike was regarding her with an intense look. Emily resisted the urge to shuffle on her chair. A persistent throbbing was starting between her legs, and wriggling seemed to make it worse.

"Chambers should have said something at the beginning." Mike said quietly. "I don't like secrets."

"And you know why I couldn't say anything before. Don't let us go through all this again."

"Okay, fine." Mike huffed and raised his hands. "I'll concede on that. For now. But no more secrets from now on, got it?"

"Got it."

Emily didn't have any problem with that. Lying for as long as she had about who she was had been incredibly difficult, and not doing it with just one person was refreshing. Emily hoped she could get things back to how they were from before it all went tits up.

Or as much as she could. Nothing was going to be completely different. Emily had hated Union in the beginning. It was on the other side of the country and was a place where Emily would never be expected to go to. She wouldn't be here, otherwise. But now, Union had grown on her. It wasn't as bad as Emily had thought. Union was actually a decent place.

The fact that she had a gorgeous boss who was currently in front of her had nothing to do with it.

Liar.

Mike rose and took Emily's empty plate. Then he limped over with the two plates to the dishwasher. His limp was looking more pronounced and he was barely hiding a grimace. Emily sat up.

"How's your knee?"

"Sore. I was supposed to be resting it instead of walking over our acreage to check things through."

Now Emily felt bad. She should have told Mike that she would take the safe house. Much as she hated being confined with a couple of squaddies she didn't know hovering over her, at least they weren't suffering with their limbs. Mike was fit, certainly more than she expected, but his knee was giving him problems. She should have been more considerate about his health.

"I should have taken the safe house."

Mike snorted.

"Not a chance."

"Excuse me?"

"You wouldn't be able to cope with that. I'd expect you to get arrested for volatile behavior if you were stuck in a safe house." Mike opened the dishwasher and put the plates in. "I know you well enough to know that you would seriously struggle with that."

"What do you call this?" Emily gestured at her surroundings. "This place is great, but it's essentially the same. I just have different guards."

Mike straightened up and frowned at her.

"You're not used to letting people help you out, are you? You want to be the one in charge, no control given to anyone else. Not even your boss."

"Too damn right." Emily rose to her feet. "I got to where I am through fucking hard work. I didn't use my father or my grandfather's connections to get into the army, and I certainly didn't ask my brother for help. I got to where I am because it was all me."

Mike's eyes drifted over her face.

"There's nothing wrong with allowing other people to help. And there's nothing wrong with admitting when you're way in over your head."

"I'm not in over my head!"

"Are you not?" Mike advanced on her, still limping but less so. "What do you call being in a city on the other side of the country under a different name for several months?"

Emily had no answer to that. But she wasn't going to back down. She advanced on him, prodding Mike in the chest.

"Get this through your head, Wilson. I'm a soldier, and a damn fine one.

And I'm going to get myself out of this, with or without your help. So you can argue with me about keeping myself safe against actually finding the fucker who put me here in the first fucking place. I can't do both, and you certainly can't."

"You certainly got something right."

"What?"

Mike grabbed her wrist, his eyes flaring as he tugged her closer, making her fall against his chest.

"You're damn fine."

His kiss was bruising, sucking the air out of Emily's lungs. Emily gasped, and Mike's tongue dived into her mouth, sucking at her tongue. Fuck, he could kiss. Intense and fierce, which was Mike all over. One hand gripped her wrist against his chest and the other wrapped around her waist, cupping her backside in a firm squeeze.

Emily loved a man who could dominate. She loved a man who could take charge of her. And Mike was ticking all the boxes.

She pressed her free hand to his chest, curling her fingers into his shirt as she scraped her teeth against his lower lip. Mike stiffened, and then he growled against her mouth, which had Emily shivering all over. Releasing her wrist, his hands closed over her backside and lifted her off the floor. Emily gripped onto his shoulders as her legs wrapped around his waist, moaning when Mike thrust against her core, pressing her hips against his erection.

Fuck, he was hard. And huge. Emily shuddered, throwing her head back in a loud moan. Mike's mouth went to her neck, sucking in the skin over her carotid artery.

"I'd say you were damn fine, Emily." His voice practically rumbled through his whole body. "I'd happily show you how damn fine you are."

"Mike..."

"No talking." Mike spun around, pressing Emily against the fridge. "I'm done talking."

He kissed her again, his hips thrusting. Emily whimpered as he hit the right spot where her clit was. It sent shocks of pleasure rippling through her body. Holy shit. They weren't even naked and Emily was about to go off like a rocket. If Mike kept thrusting against her body like that, Emily was going to be red-hot.

If only she could get these damn clothes off.

The sudden sound of a car alarm had both of them freezing. Mike drew back with a muffled curse.

"Shit." Easing Emily to the floor, he leaned her against the fridge. "Wait here. I'll go and check it out."

"Hell, no." Emily protested. "I'm going with you."

"No, you're staying here. And that's an order."

Emily's eyes narrowed, her mouth curling into a scowl. But she didn't argue, simply staring at him as she tried to get her breath back. Her legs were struggling to get any leverage.

Mike grunted, his expression saying he didn't expect Emily to stay, and he hurried out into the hall. That was when Emily saw the gun tucked into the back of his jeans. He was armed the whole time? Where the fuck was her weapon?

Emily counted to ten, expecting to hear gunfire or some shouting. But all she could hear was the car alarm. Nothing else.

Now she was beginning to panic. Had Mike been jumped? Was Marsden in the house?

Ignoring what Mike had ordered, Emily hurried into the hall and through the house, bursting out into the carport. Mike was there, but he hadn't been attacked. He was upright, his gun out as he stood next to her car.

Or more rather, standing next to the dead body draped across the hood of the car.

#

Susan Grey was dead. Marsden had managed to find his girlfriend. According to Emily, when Mike had managed to get it out of her, Susan had gone under the radar when Marsden broke out of jail. Nobody knew where she had gone, and Emily had thought Susan would be safe. Clearly, she wasn't.

Somehow, Marsden had found his ex-girlfriend, killed her and brought her to South Carolina to dump in front of the place Emily was hiding at. And from the decomposition of Susan's body, she had been dead for a while. At least two weeks.

Now Mike was worried. Not only did Marsden know exactly where Emily was, but he had managed to sneak past all of the alarms and traps Mike had set. He hadn't heard anything until the car alarm went off due to a nicely aimed shot at the back windshield. How had Marsden managed to get past all of his traps? Did he have someone watching Emily at all times? Or was it him watching Emily?

Maybe he should have made Emily go to the safe house. At least Marsden wouldn't be able to get close. Then again, Marsden was a soldier. And a top one, from what his file said after Mike asked Scott for a sneaky peek. He could get past anything he wanted, given half a chance. It was what made him popular in Afghanistan as a scout and sniper before he became an MP.

Although how much of that was Marsden having friends in the right places and simply letting him through was anyone's guess.

The police arrived quickly and they were equally stunned at the body on the car. Mike had no real answers for them. None that he was cleared for, anyway. He had to play the innocent, confused citizen who had no idea why there was a dead woman's body on his land.

Emily was no help. Mike had hustled her back inside as soon as he saw her. If Marsden was still around, he wasn't about to let her get shot. Emily was white as a sheet as she stared at Susan's body. For a moment, Mike thought she was about to cry and he had to struggle not to pull her into his arms to comfort her.

The few intense moments he finally had her in his arms felt like a million years ago.

Mike dealt with the cops, the crime scene officers and the coroner. All of them kept looking at him like it was his fault, but Mike simply played the confused homeowner, claiming ignorance. For the most part, he really was ignorant.

Chambers was not going to like this. He was going to demand that Emily went into a safe house, yet again, and that this was a bad idea. But Mike knew he wouldn't be able to let go of Emily. Not now.

You just had to kiss her, didn't you? You idiot. Now you're going to be thinking with the wrong head.

It was about two hours before the last cop car left with a promise that a detective was going to come over to discuss what had happened and to take a statement. Mike was not looking forward to it. That meant more lying and hoping that Emily, if she was asked for a statement as well, wouldn't give anything away.

Because after what she had seen, Mike wouldn't be surprised if Emily gave in and told the cops everything. Karen was dead, and now Susan. Emily had been attacked herself. It was clear that she was a target. Marsden had put two dead bodies at her front door to make a point. That was toying with Emily, making her freak out to come out into the open.

That was a point. Maybe Marsden didn't really know that Emily was here. Maybe he had put Susan here because she knew it would get back to Emily. If he did his research, he would know who Emily worked for. Karen had been left at the restaurant and now Susan at Mike's house.

Mike didn't know what to think anymore. Everything was a mess in his head. He couldn't begin to imagine how Emily was thinking.

Once the last car had disappeared, Mike went past inside. Emily was sitting on the couch, her cell phone on the coffee table. She was hunched over, arms wrapped around her middle as she stared straight ahead. She looked like a shadow of her former self, a faraway expression in her eyes.

"Emily?"

Emily didn't react. Mike limped over and sat beside her. He touched her back, and Emily didn't pull away. He realized that she was trembling.

"They've gone now. Did you call Chambers?"

"I did." Emily's voice was soft, almost a whisper. "To say he's furious is an understatement. He thinks I should be going into a safe house or move to another part of the country by midnight."

Mike's chest tightened. That meant Emily would disappear again. He wasn't allowing that.

"What do you think?"

"I don't want to go, but…" Emily licked her lips. "I shouldn't be here. Two dead bodies, one at your business and one at your home. Marsden knows where I am, and he's killing everyone involved in the trial. I seem to be the prime target and he's taunting me." She started to rock. "I can't stay here if he's going to come after me here."

She's not going anywhere. I can protect her better than those jarheads can. Mike slid his hand up her back and cupped the back of her neck.

"There will be none of that, Lieutenant. No defeatist talk here."

"But Karen and Susan…"

"Were left at places that have my name on it because Marsden knows I'm connected to you. He might not even know that you're here, it could be a hint that he can get to anyone, or it's a way to draw you out so he can kill you."

Emily snorted.

"You don't sound like you believe that."

"Not particularly, but it's an option." Mike tightened his grip, urging Emily to lean into him. "I only know that I can protect you. You're not going anywhere, and I won't let Marsden do anything to you."

"He got past your defences." Emily pointed out. "What are the chances he gets into the house?"

"Not a chance."

Mike wouldn't let it happen. The house was even more tightly secured than the grounds. And with the weaponry he had, Marsden would find himself in a gunfight he wasn't prepared for. Mike would make sure of it.

Marsden was not getting Emily.

But what happened when Marsden was captured? What happened then? Would Emily go back to where she came from? Would she leave Union for good? Mike felt the knot tighten in his stomach. The thought of Emily leaving did not sit well with him.

Would he be able to persuade her to stay? Mike wasn't sure.

"I'm going to check the perimeter." Mike rose to his feet. "Secure everything. Put the alarm on behind me, will you? Code is six-four-two-nine."

"Okay." Emily rose to her feet, her arms still wrapped around her. "You won't take long, will you?"

"Hopefully not." Mike leaned over and kissed her forehead. "Make yourself at home. Do whatever you can to take your mind off what happened. Focus your energy onto something else."

"Is that an order, Sergeant?"

Mike grinned.

"Definitely. I'll be right back."

With Emily standing so close to him, looking up at him with that expression that made his heart hurt, Mike knew if he stayed any longer he would be carrying on what he had started in the kitchen. That wasn't a good idea. He had to keep her safe first.

Somehow, he managed to turn and walk out of the room.

Chapter Thirteen

After setting the alarm behind Mike once he left the house, Emily felt at a loss. Normally, she was so sure about what she needed to do. What the next step was. And this time she felt like she was floundering.

Her parents had told her that she needed to be strong enough, to be independent, to be successful as a soldier. If she wasn't, she was going to get walked all over. Emily liked to think she was strong. Independent. Good at her job. But her parents had also taught her something else, something Emily often forgot about.

Swallow your pride when you need to. And Emily hadn't done that.

Maybe she needed to do this now. She had a criminal who had a hard-on for her and he was taunting her. Karen's body had turned up yesterday and then that evening Emily had been attacked. Now Susan's body was on its way to the morgue. Did that mean Marsden was going to come after her tonight?

He had managed to get through Mike's alarms. There was a good chance that the bastard could slip through again.

Her confidence was wavering. Marsden was proving to be more slippery than they thought. Two strong, capable women were dead. And Emily was top of his list.

She didn't want to let him take the chance. But she was getting so tired of running. Emily didn't run. The only reason she agreed to going into hiding was after someone shot at her parents while Emily was recuperating with them after her stay in hospital. Everyone she cared about would be a target unless Emily disappeared. Nobody hurt her family if Emily had anything to do with it.

Marsden was going to pay. If she got the chance, Emily was going to put her gun between his eyes and pull the trigger. He was not going to keep her running anymore.

Sitting on the couch waiting for Mike to come back in wasn't helping her. Emily felt antsy just sitting there staring at the walls. She needed to do something, but what? Pacing around the living room, she cast her eye over the bookcases. The books looked interesting, but Emily didn't feel calm enough to sit down and read. The same with the DVDs. She needed to do something active, something to take her mind off what was going on. Exercise was just not going to cut it.

Then Emily saw the video games. All lined up on the middle shelf. Curious, Emily had a look over them. A few shooter games, which was no surprise, but most of them were horror. Emily had a few of her own back home, but she hadn't been able to take her PS4 and games with her. One of her friends had picked up a few clothes. She had needed to get a new laptop, new toiletries and had a new bank account with a certain amount of money along with a new passport and driving license. Everything was brand new, and there was not enough in there to justify getting a new PS4 and the games to go with it. After all, she had other things to pay for first and there wasn't enough to treat herself to one, even with a job.

If they were to put her into hiding, they could at least have transferred her money over. That would make Emily more than comfortable.

Hopefully, Mike wouldn't mind if she fired up the PS4 and had a few games. She needed something to take her mind off what was happening, and losing herself in a virtual world would go some way to doing that.

Emily selected *Dead Space* and popped it into the PS4. After a few tweaks finding out how the TV worked, she started playing. Shooting alien creatures and jumping at shadows was somehow very therapeutic. Emily found herself lost in the world in deep space, navigating her way through the derelict ship trying to figure out how to get it going again while she searched for the character's girlfriend.

Her parents thought she was mad to play games like this, especially at her age. But Emily simply smiled and shrugged.

"Having fun, are you?"

Emily shrieked and dropped the control, which resulted in her character getting killed. She spun around and saw Mike in the doorway, watching her with a slight smile. Amusement sparkled in his eyes. Biting her lip, Emily scrambled to pause the game.

"How did you get in? I thought I was supposed to let you in."

"I let myself in and disabled the alarm." Mike nodded at the TV. "With the noise coming from that, I'm surprised you could hear anything else."

Emily groaned. She rose to her feet.

"I'm sorry."

"No need." Mike pushed himself off the doorway. "After everything that's happened, no one's going to get upset with you for wanting to escape."

Why did she have to blush? Just the mere presence of Mike had Emily's whole body feeling like she was on fire. She could feel her nipples tightening and rub against her bra as Mike approached her. Emily was taken back to when she had been up against the fridge with Mike's cock rubbing between her legs, and she had to bite back a moan.

If he touched her now, she was going to be putty in his hands.

"I..." Emily looked anywhere but at Mike, focusing on the games console. "I'm sorry for using your stuff. I just needed something to do, and this..."

"I'm not going to get upset about that." Mike gestured at the PS4. "I haven't played in a while with everything going on, and Prudence doesn't get much use out of it. She's not into video games."

"She doesn't take after her dad, then?"

"Not like that, no."

Then Emily remembered Prudence. She was out right now. What if Marsden saw her and used her as a bargaining chip? She began to panic.

"Is Prudence okay? Is Marsden goes after her..."

"I've already spoken to Prudence." Mike held up her hand, stilling her fears. "She's going to spend the night at a friend's. She'll come back sometime tomorrow."

That was something. But it didn't ease many of Emily's fears.

"Marsden can still use her against me. If he does know I'm here and that Prudence is going to come back…"

"Emily." Mike laid her hands on her shoulders. "It's going to be okay. Marsden is trying to show that he's clever, but he's not. He's going to get caught, and you're going to be safe. Just take a deep breath and let it out. Marsden will not hurt you. I will make sure of it."

He will make sure of it. All the other words went out of Emily's head as soon as he touched her. His palms were warm, seeping through her jumper. She wanted to lean into him, wrap her arms around him and sink into his warmth. She just needed someone else right now.

She wanted Mike.

It would be so easy to rely on him. He's solid and loyal. He would always be there.

"Can I ask you a personal question, Emily?"

Emily blinked. Mike's hands drifted over her shoulders and down her arms. His fingers brushed against hers, and Emily felt the electricity trickle up her arms. Had it gotten a little warmer now? Emily swallowed.

"It depends on what the question is."

"Is…" Mike hesitated. "Is there anyone special in your life? Like a boyfriend or…a husband?"

Emily stared. He was asking that now after he had kissed her like he was drowning?

"Why are you asking?"

"I just…" Mike grimaced. "I'm going to plead the fifth on that one. Other than to say I want to know I'm not overstepping the boundaries set up."

Emily snorted.

"You think I would have kissed you as I did earlier if I was in a relationship?"

"There's something called adrenaline." Mike groaned and pulled away. "I guess I'm not good at this. I just…"

"You just what?"

But Mike didn't answer. He turned away and went to the window, shoving his hands into his pockets. There had to be a reason for asking. Emily waited.

She could wait.

"I was in a relationship when you first came here. I'm sure you know that." Mike didn't turn around as he spoke. "She's with the US attorney's office. And I caught her cheating. She thought it was no big deal, but for me that doesn't work. When I'm with someone, they have me for the whole haul, and I expect the same." His shoulders hunched over. "I won't be taken for a mug."

Now Emily understood. He had been hurt before. Trying to find love again after his wife died had to be tough, and it knocked a person back when it didn't work. She was starting to see the vulnerable side of Mike. He just wanted someone to love him fully.

Could she do that for him?

Absolutely. I can do that.

Emily approached him, pressing a hand to his back. Mike stilled, but he didn't move away.

"I'm not married." She murmured. "I'm single. I did have a boyfriend, but he was linked to Marsden. I had to break things off when he was defending Marsden's actions." She took a breath. "I also have suspicions that he helped Marsden leave prison and get into my house."

Mike turned and stared at her.

"You serious?"

"Nothing concrete, so he's only been questioned and let go. But I know in my gut he had something to do with it."

Mike's eyes narrowed.

"Was this Houghton-Leathers your boyfriend, by any chance?"

Emily nodded. Mike grunted.

"It would explain his comments when he came by. Now I get why you were freaked out that he was looking for you."

"He saw me back when the Super Bowl was happening. I told him to forget I was there and that Emily was dead."

"Well, he didn't get the message." Mike frowned. "Do you think he's helping Marsden with this?"

"I would not be surprised if his name came up." Emily realized that her hand had moved when Mike turned around. Now her hand was resting against his chest, her fingers feeling his heartbeat under her touch. "But I can't bring myself to trust anyone like that again. After what's happened, it's not easy."

"I understand." Mike laid his hand over hers, his touch gentle. "Do you trust me, Emily?"

Emily didn't even need to think. She had trusted him from the start. Mike had never lied to her and he had always had her best interests at heart. He was like that with everyone. Underneath his gruff, staunch attitude at work, Mike cared. And he did it with everything he had.

It wouldn't take much to fall for him.

Maybe I already have.

Emily cupped his jaw.

"I trust you."

"Good."

Mike slid his hand into her hair and tilted her head up, pressing his mouth to hers.

#

This was unlike the kiss before. It was soft, sweet. And it still made Emily's body feel like she was being licked by flames. Everything about it built her desire as much as it had when he was taking charge.

Mike took his time tasting her mouth. He slid his tongue across the seam of her lips, nibbling at her lower lip before tilting her head and slowly deepening the kiss. Emily sighed and leaned into him, pressing her hands against his chest as his arm wrapped around her waist. His erection pressed against her belly, and Emily whimpered. She was close to just dropping to her knees and pulling his jeans down to touch his cock. Put her mouth around him and savor how he tasted. The thought made her groan.

Mike's hand cupped her backside and he squeezed, lifting her up on her tiptoes. Emily gripped his shoulders and tried to clamber up his body. This wasn't close enough. She needed more. A lot more.

She felt Mike's chuckle rumble through his chest, smiling against her mouth.

"You're eager, aren't you?"

110

"Guilty." Emily reached between them and rubbed his erection, causing Mike to groan. "I'm not the only one who's eager."

"I've been eager since you walked into my business." Mike thrust against her hand. His hand in her hair drifted down her neck and cupped her breast, the roughness of his touch making Emily gasp. "Just so you know, I take charge. I'm not a gentle lover."

Not a gentle lover. Perfect. Emily arched into his hand, her fingers tightening around his erection.

"I don't want gentle. I want you." She grabbed his head and tugged him down. "Now."

Mike growled. This time, his kiss was not gentle. He plundered her mouth, hauling Emily almost off her feet as he thrust against her hand. Emily tried to hold on with one hand, only to find herself wobbling. Mike caught her before she fell and hoisted her up into his arms, her legs wrapping around his waist. Then he shoved her jumper up, pushing her bra off her breasts. He sucked her nipple into his mouth, his teeth scraping against her breast. Emily shuddered as pleasure rippled through her. Holy shit, she wouldn't need much before she was screaming. The roughness of how he took her breast, the tight grip on her backside as he thrust against her core, it was incredible.

She needed this.

She needed him.

"Mike…I…" She managed to drag her head up, making him look at her. His eyes were dark, hunger blazing. Emily loved that look on him. "Take me to bed. I want you."

Mike's jaw tightened. His hands flexed on her backside.

"I'm not letting go now, Emily. Make sure you're certain."

"I'm certain." Emily dug her nails into his scalp. "Don't stall, Mike. Now."

Mike buried his face into her neck with a chuckle.

"I knew you were eager."

He left the room and managed to get up the stairs. Emily clung to him, hoping that he didn't trip up and send both of them sprawling. Instead of going into her bedroom at the end of the hall, Mike turned to a room on his left, stepping into his room. Then he fell onto the bed, kissing her like he was starving. Emily scraped her fingers through his hair, digging into his shoulders as she tightened her legs around his waist. His cock was right where she needed him, pressing against her clit through the fabric.

She needed these clothes to go away.

Mike broke the kiss suddenly, breathing heavily. The desire in his face had Emily whimpering. He started to pull back, but Emily tightened her hold on him.

"Don't go."

"I'm not going anywhere." Mike eased her legs apart, shifting down the bed. "I'm not going until I've made you scream my name at least twice."

"Optimistic, aren't you?" Emily panted as he kissed down her belly. "I'm lucky if I come once."

"Then I've got a challenge in front of me." Mike flashed her a grin. "I love a challenge."

Then he pressed his mouth against her clit through her jeans. Emily almost shot off the bed. Fuck. The pressure of her jeans and his mouth, teeth rubbing through the denim over her sensitive clit, was almost too much for her. Emily had never come during foreplay. It just didn't stimulate her enough. But now Mike was throwing all that out the window.

Mike pulled away sharply, leaving Emily gasping, and he reached for his shirt.

"Get your clothes off." He growled. "Get them off and on your hands and knees."

Emily found herself smiling as she managed to sit up.

"Back in the army, are we, Sergeant?"

"Did I ask you to talk?"

Emily had to stop herself from giggling even as a thrill went through her. This was what she wanted. A man who could take charge. Mike was just that. She tugged her clothes off, tossing them onto the floor and getting onto her hands and knees. Her pussy throbbed enough to make her whimper as she watched Mike take off his socks and then drop his shirt, revealing a washboard stomach with muscles that looked like he had been carved out of stone. Then he unbuttoned his jeans and pushed them down his thighs, his boxers going with them.

Emily's mouth went dry when she saw his cock. Wow. Long and thick, it stood up proudly from his groin, almost touching his navel. Emily found herself reaching between her legs to touch her clit. The build-up was getting too much.

"Don't." Mike's sharp command stopped her. "Don't touch yourself. Get up on your knees, hands behind your back."

Emily knew she was trembling as she rose up onto her knees, locking her fingers together behind her back. Mike's eyes travelled over her body, slowly licking his lips. He growled and beckoned her towards him with a crook of his finger. Emily shuffled closer, almost at the edge of the bed. Mike reached out and slid a hand down her chest, cupping her breast.

"You've got a gorgeous body, Emily." He flicked her nipple with his finger, making Emily. "So beautiful." Then his hand travelled lower. "So hot."

His fingers brushed through her curls, and circled her clit without touching it. Emily shivered, her hips jerking. Mike gripped her hip with one hand, keeping her still, while his other hand moved further and brushed over her pussy lips. He groaned.

"You're so wet already. I love how responsive you are." He lowered his neck and licked up her neck to her ear. "I can't wait to see how responsive you'll be with my cock inside you."

"Mike…"

Emily was shaking, so close to the edge already. And he had barely touched her. Then Mike's hands disappearing, leaving her swaying. He began to press down on her shoulders.

"Bend over. Grip the edge of the bed if you need to."

Emily obeyed, gripping the edge of the mattress as her body threatened to tilt her forward and onto the floor. Mike's cock bumped her chin. Emily couldn't stop herself from giving the head a lick. Mike groaned.

"So eager. You'll have what you want." He positioned his cock against her lips, gently pushing. "Take me into your mouth. Let my cock fuck your mouth."

Dirty talk had never been so arousing. Emily opened her mouth and Mike thrust gently inside. He was wide, very wide, and Emily could barely get her lips around him. There was no way she would get all of him into her mouth. Couldn't she take him in completely?

Her pussy clenched. *Oh, hell, yes. I can take him.*

"Fuck, Emily." Mike pulled back and thrust again, one hand slipping through her hair. "Your mouth is amazing. Keep sucking my cock like that."

He thrust gently, easing more of his cock inside. Then the tip bumped against the back of Emily's throat, and she almost gagged. Mike eased back and waited, his hand smoothing her hair. Then he started thrusting again, not pushing too much. Emily tightened her lips around him, using her teeth to scrape against the soft underside of his shaft. That had Mike moaning.

"Fuck!"

Emily's body was on fire. She had never been so submissive before, and she had never been so close to coming herself without being touched. She began to bob her head, meeting Mike's thrusts with her own. His cock bumped her throat again, but Emily relaxed and took more of him in. She wanted this. She wanted more.

Mike leaned over her, his hand running over her butt cheek. Then he shoved two fingers into her pussy. Emily screamed around his cock, her muscles clamping down on him. Mike groaned.

"Shit, Emily. You're so tight." His fingers thrust in faster. "I can't wait to fuck you."

She wanted to be fucked now. She needed to be fucked. Emily sucked harder on Mike's cock, feeling his fingers pump in and out of her pussy. He stretched her, built the pleasure to a high that threatened to explode. Emily whimpered and wriggled her hips. She needed to come. It was too much.

Then Mike tapped her clit, and Emily shattered. She screamed around his cock, unable to move as Mike pinned her with his hand firmly on her hip. He fucked her mouth with his cock and he fucked her pussy with his fingers, worrying her clit as Emily shuddered through her orgasm. It was too much. But she wanted more. So much more.

She was almost collapsing onto the bed when Mike slowly pulled his fingers out. He straightened up, sliding his still very hard cock from her mouth. Then Emily was being lifted upright. Mike gathered her into his arms and kissed her, a sensual kiss that had Emily's desire building up again.

"God, Emily." Mike cupped her breast as he nuzzled her neck. "You felt so good."

"I...Mike..."

Mike chuckled, the vibration against her neck making Emily shudder.

"Speechless for once?"

"Doesn't happen...often." Emily tugged his head up. "Don't get a big head over it."

"Too late." Mike took her hand and pressed it over his cock. "It's already very big." He kissed her thoroughly, palming her backside. "I need to be inside you. Now."

"I've got the coil in." Emily cupped his face in her hands. "Latex allergy. And I'm clean."

"I'm clean, too." Mike's eyes darkened. "God, to take you like that..."

"Then do it." Emily kissed him. "I want this."

That was when there was an explosion that rocked the whole house.

Chapter Fourteen

Mike dived to the bed and covered Emily with his body. The whole house shook with the explosion, the noise ringing in his ears. What the hell had just happened?

All thoughts of sex went out of his head as he rolled off Emily and grabbed for his jeans.

"Get dressed."

"What happened?" Emily clambered off the bed, snatching up her clothes. "What was that bang?"

"I don't know. I'm going to find out."

Mike managed to get his half-erect cock into his jeans, wincing as he zipped up. Emily tugged her jeans on, slipping her jumper on. No underwear. *You shouldn't be thinking about that right now!*

"Do you think it's Marsden?" Emily asked. "He can't get me out so he's trying to blow me up?"

"I have no idea right now." Mike went to his wardrobe. "But I'm not going to let him destroy my home."

He opened up the box at the bottom of the wardrobe, bringing out two handguns. He loaded both and held one out to Emily. She took it and fed one bullet into the chamber. Her expression was blank now, but anger was blazing in her eyes.

"I hope it's Marsden." She said. "I'm going to kill him."

Mike didn't doubt it. Emily was wound tightly like a bowstring. Seeing Marsden was going to make her snap.

Not if I have anything to do with it.

Mike could feel Emily close behind him as they slowly descended the stairs. There was no point in telling Emily to stay where she was. She would follow him regardless. And she was hardly defenceless.

Gone was the warm, delectable Emily from moments ago. This Emily was cold and hard. Professional.

Seeing that was more of a turn-on than the warm Emily.

Your head is still back in the bedroom. Not a good place right now, soldier.

At least Emily was behind him. Or it would be more of a distraction.

They reached the bottom of the stairs. The front door was broken in, half-off its hinges. Glass and splinters littered the floor. Still keeping his gun up, Mike crouched and reached for a pair of his sneakers, passing Emily her shoes.

"I'll check the carport." He whispered, shoving his feet into his footwear. "You check the back."

"Got it."

Emily slid her shoes on and came off the stairs, keeping her gun up and pointed down the hall as she headed towards the kitchen. Mike straightened up and went out the front into the carport. The car his insurance had let him use was still there, but it had police tape wrapped around it. There was no sign of anyone close by.

But a closer inspection of the door and the area outside showed fragments of a bomb. Shrapnel just littered the ground. Someone had detonated what looked to be a homemade device right outside his front door. What would be the point of that? Blow them to pieces if they opened the door?

Or to distract them to the front while he got in elsewhere?

Mike's heart almost stopped when he heard a gunshot inside. Then there was some shouting.

"Emily!"

Mike ran inside, charging through into the kitchen. Emily was pressed up against the kitchen table, almost bent over backwards, wrestling with someone dressed in black. The gun was between them, almost pointed at Emily's face. Then her knee came up and caught the guy between the legs. Her attacker cried out and jerked, the gun jumping between them. Emily pulled it away and punched him in the face, knocking him sideways. She jerked out of the way rolling across the floor and coming up with her gun pointed at his head.

"You value your life, Marsden, you stay down." She snarled.

For a moment, Mike thought the guy was going to comply. He kept his sights on Marsden's head, watching as his eyes burned fury in Emily's direction. He thought this idiot was actually going to back down. But instead, their intruder snarled and launched himself at Emily.

Mike fired one shot. His body jerked and Mike watched as Marsden fell back, slumping on the floor with a grunt. He pressed a hand to his stomach, and Mike saw the blood pooling between his fingers.

Emily was staring at Mike, her eyes wide. Mike ignored her, stepping towards the man who had broken into their house. Only hours after tossing a body practically onto his front lawn and the bastard was trying again.

Crouching, with his gun pressed into the intruder's side, Mike found a gun tucked into his pants. Withdrawing it, he rose to his feet and backed away.

"You try to go for another weapon and I'll make sure the next shot is a kill shot."

Marsden snarled at him.

"Fucking bastard! I'll kill you once I'm done with her."

"Focus on keeping yourself from bleeding out and not on talking." Mike glanced at Emily. She was still staring at him. "You okay, Emily?"

"You...you shot him."

Emily sounded dazed. Mike growled.

"Now is not the time, Lieutenant! Go and call 911. This guy needs an ambulance. And let Chambers know."

"I...okay."

Still looking bewildered, Emily hurried out of the room. Mike focused on Marsden, who was now pressing both of his hands against his belly. Both hands were getting coated with blood. Marsden's breathing was beginning to sound like he was wheezing.

"You...I really will kill you, Wilson. No one should protect snitches."

"And no one should abuse their position of power." Mike shot back. "You did the wrong thing. You were going to pay for that."

"No one tells on me." Marsden's breathing was getting more shallow. "And they found out the hard way."

Even shot and bleeding all over Mike's floor, he was still defiant. Mike moved just in reach and crouched, not moving the gun from Marsden's face. Marsden's eyes flickered to the gun and back up to Mike's face, which Mike shook his head.

"Don't even try it. You may have youth on your side, but I'm not the one with a bullet to the gut. You won't be able to handle me."

"You want a bet?"

"Don't even try it." Mike reached out and grabbed at the balaclava. "And if you're going to threaten me, I'm going to see your face."

Marsden growled and tried to get away, but he fell back with a groan. Mike took a firmer hold on the balaclava, and gave it a tug. It came off easily, and then Mike was staring into the face of Eddie Marsden. A face he recognized. One he had not expected to see glaring back at him.

"Holy shit." Mike stared. He couldn't help himself. "Will?"

"What?" Emily was in the doorway, her cell phone in her hand. "You know him?"

"Will Carruthers. He's been coming into the bar since the start of the year."

Emily's eyes widened. She stared at Marsden, who was now sneering at her.

"You knew where I was the whole time?"

"Since around New Year." Marsden smirked. "You thought you were safe, O'Rourke. You were never safe. I was just saving you for one of the last ones."

"Because I arrested you for doing the wrong thing?"

"For arresting me at all." Marsden's lip curled into a snarl. "Nobody gets away with arresting me. Especially a woman."

Mike felt like he had been hit over the head. So, all of this was for nothing? Marsden had known where Emily was almost from the start. The bastard had been simply toying with them. Emily had never been safe at all. God only knows how long Marsden had been laughing at her.

And to walk into his restaurant and stick to the bar while Emily was working? That was just brazen.

"You murdered those women and then dumped them on Emily's doorstep to taunt her?"

"She knows she can't get away from me." Marsden's mouth twitched in a smug smile. "And who said I killed them? I don't need to kill anyone. Except her," he flashed a scowl in Emily's direction, "I'll enjoy killing her."

Emily growled. Mike shot her a look and pointed towards the front door.

"Go and wait for the ambulance, Lieutenant. That's an order."

"But…"

"Go!"

Emily looked like she was about to argue, but she decided against it. With one last glance at Marsden, she backed out of the room. Marsden sniggered.

"Does she follow orders in the bedroom as well? Darryl says she's not exactly inventive."

Mike snarled and pulled out a chair, lifting himself into it.

"Shut up." He pointed the gun at Marsden's face. "You're going to stay quiet until the cops come here to arrest you."

"You're not going to help me?" Marsden held up a hand. "I'm shot and I'm bleeding out."

"You shouldn't have blown up my front door and broken in to get at Emily." Mike snapped. He shifted back so Marsden could grab his legs. "Now shut up. I'm sure the cops are going to love to know what happened here."

Marsden scowled. But he did shut up. Whether it was from Mike's order or from blood loss, Mike didn't know, but the silence was welcoming.

#

"Where's Marsden?"

Emily looked up. Then jumped to her feet. Chambers was in the doorway, his hair saying that he had literally rolled out of bed. She had called him as soon as she finished calling for an ambulance. Not that she wanted to; she would prefer to call the coroner.

If she had been allowed to shoot Marsden as she wanted. But Mike had got there first. Had he known her intentions? Emily wished she had been quicker on the draw.

Don't think it would have made you feel any better, because it wouldn't.
I should've been allowed to find out.

"He's been taken away in an ambulance. The cops are with him." Emily rubbed her away, very aware that she wasn't wearing a bra in front of her commanding officer. "I contacted Fort Jackson and they're sending some men to guard him when he undergoes surgery."

Chambers arched an eyebrow.

"Did you shoot him?"

"No, I didn't."

Emily didn't say anything more. Chambers searched her face, seeming to be unsatisfied with her answer. But he simply grunted and ran a hand through his hair.

"Well, I'll make sure he's put under constant watch with some extra charges pressed onto him. Once he's able to travel, he's going back to Tacoma. Then he won't see the light of day." Chambers spread his hands. "Then this will all be over."

"All be over." Emily murmured.

That didn't give her much relief. Not as she expected. Instead, something niggled away in the back of her mind. Most of the pieces were there, but they weren't quite fitting. Emily had spent the last half-hour sitting on the couch, away from the scene as Mike dealt with the emergency services and they took Marsden away, trying to figure out where it was going wrong. But she had nothing definitive. Just a lot of ifs, buts and maybes.

That was enough for her.

Chambers frowned.

"Emily?"

"Hmm?"

"You've gone quiet on me. I said it's over and you had a strange look on your face." He tilted his head to the side as he regarded her. "You don't think this is over, do you?"

"No, I don't." Emily rubbed at her belly. "Something in my gut says this isn't done. I'm glad Marsden's caught now, but..."

"But what?" Chambers folded his arms. "Emily, you were the one who was complaining about being stuck in hiding while Marsden was running around. We've finally got him. What's wrong now?"

"I don't think he was doing this alone. Hear me out," Emily held up a hand as Chambers started to protest, "Marsden had to have help to get out of jail. He's good, but he's not that good. Karen and Susan were nowhere near Union, and yet they turned up? I'm pretty sure Marsden hasn't been able to go to their homes and kill them before lugging them here."

"You believe someone else is pulling strings?" Chambers murmured. "One of his employers helping him out?"

"Or he has someone else working with him. Someone who watches me while Marsden goes to kill Karen and Susan or the other way around."

It was only a gut feeling, no definite proof, but Emily was certain about this. Marsden couldn't have done this on his own. He wasn't that independent. He always had to have someone around him to do the dirty work while he looked like the brains. Everyone in the office had rolled his eyes at his behavior, but Marsden simply shrugged and walked away. The credit was everything to him.

"Assuming he has a partner," Chambers said, "who would it be?"

"An old business partner, former squaddie, maybe even family." Emily swallowed as her main suspect floated into the forefront of her mind. "Or it could be Darryl."

Chamber's eyebrows almost shot up to his hairline.

"You think your ex helped him with these murders?"

"I think he had something to do with it. He knew where I was way back during the Super Bowl. And he did come into the restaurant the same day Karen was found and asked for me."

"He came in and you didn't tell me?"

Emily winced.

"A lot has gone on over the last couple of days."

"You're telling me." Chambers scowled. "It's a long shot, but I'll speak to his CO about it. I hope to God you're wrong."

He left the room, shaking his head. Emily ran her hands through her hair. She was exhausted. Her hands were still shaking. Her gun had been taken from her by Mike, who said he would sort everything out, but she could feel it still in her grip.

She was so close to pulling the trigger, putting the end to this. Emily had dreamed many nights about killing Marsden. He had put her through hell. She had been forced to run for her own safety. No fucking way was she going to keep doing that. If he was brazen to break into an alarmed house where two squaddies were, he should expect to get shot. Preferably between the eyes than in the gut.

Mike had taken that away from her. Emily was still angry about that. But it wasn't as intense as it had been when she realized that Mike had taken charge. Again. This had been unfairly snatched from her.

But the more she thought about it, the more she realized that Mike had done the right thing. He had simply disabled Marsden, put him down but kept him alive. Emily would have just killed him. She might have been able to claim self-defence and it would have been put down as justifiable.

Could she live with herself afterwards? Emily had killed before, when she was in Afghanistan, but it had always left her feeling sick, the guilt there and refusing to budge. She had done it as part of her job, making sure those causing chaos were put down. But it didn't make her feel any better.

Mike must have known that. Even if it would have been satisfying, that wouldn't have lasted long.

"Hey."

Emily looked up. Mike was walking into the room. He looked worn out, his eyes hollowed out. He looked like he had aged ten years.

Emily didn't hesitate. She met him halfway and ran into his arms. Mike wrapped her into a tight embrace, burying his face into her hair with a sigh. Emily felt the tension leave his body with a shudder and she hugged him tighter. Thank God he was safe. If Marsden had gone for him, Emily certainly wouldn't have sat back.

Mike meant too much for her to lose him now.

"How are you holding up?" Mike lifted her head, cupping her face in his hands. "You doing okay?"

"I think so." Emily grimaced. "I feel like I want to crash."

"I know. I'm the same." Mike kissed her forehead. "The cop cars and crime scene guys are still finishing off. They're going to want to speak to you in a moment."

"I know. What about the door?"

Mike smiled.

"I've got a friend who lives close by who does carpentry. I've given him a call and asked if he has anything. He'll be over soon to help me replace it."

That was something. Emily pressed her hands against his chest.

"Was he trying to kill us by answering the door? It seems a bit extreme."

"I think it was more of a distraction so he could get in the back. But, like you said, a little too much for what happened."

Emily was just glad neither of them were anywhere near the door. Or that Prudence had come home.

"How did he get so close? I thought you checked everywhere."

"I did. Clearly, I'm going to need to sort the security out around here." Mike frowned. "He managed to get through twice. I would like to know how he did that."

He was pissed. Emily cupped his jaw.

"We can get answers later. He's caught now."

"I suppose." Mike then lowered his head and nuzzled her cheek. "Just think if he had come a few minutes earlier."

Emily was transported to what they had been doing. She whimpered as her pussy clenched, remembering the way Mike had taken her before making her come around him.

"Oh, I would've been more than pissed." She kissed Mike's cheek. ""I'm glad he didn't try to break in a few minutes later, either."

Mike groaned. He trailed a hand down her back, settling on her hip.

"God, woman, if there weren't so many people here, I'd be taking us back to where we left off right now."

Emily shivered. She liked the sound of that. The thought of knowing people could hear them having sex close by. Mike paused.

"Do you like the thought of being heard?"

"Not normally." Emily smiled. "You seem to make me feel a lot of things

I'm not used to, Sergeant Wilson."

"Is that good or bad?"

"Oh, it's good." Emily brushed her lips over his. "Definitely good."

Mike growled. His fingers threaded through her hair.

"Emily…"

There was a loud cough behind them, causing Mike to jump away. Emily felt her face getting warm when she saw Chambers had come back into the room, looking from Mike to Emily and back again.

"Was I interrupting something here, Sergeant Wilson?"

"No, Colonel." Mike cleared his throat, keeping his back to the other man. "Just…just a debrief."

"I see."

A smile twitched at Chambers' mouth. Emily glared at him.

"Don't start, or I'm going to be telling all about what happened at that Christmas party three years ago."

Chambers winced.

"You're not going to make me forget that, are you?"

"Hell, no."

"You what?" Mike looked up. "What happened?"

"Never you mind." Chambers held up his cell phone. "I just spoke to Houghton-Leathers' CO. He wasn't impressed at being disturbed at this hour, but he became more awake when I explained. You can take Houghton-Leathers off your list of potential co-conspirators."

Emily frowned.

"Why?"

"Because he's dead." Chambers replied grimly. "His body was found in his home, on-base, drowned in the bathtub. Their pathologist is ruling it a homicide."

Emily stared. Darryl was dead? That didn't hurt her as much as she thought it would. It was like any emotions she had towards Darryl had died a long time ago.

"He…he was murdered?" She gulped. "How long has he been dead?"

"About twelve to eighteen hours, they've put down in the report."

"I saw him about eighteen hours ago in the restaurant asking for Emily." Mike put in. "He was certainly alive and kicking then."

"That would be about right. Records at the gate have him clocking in just before seven, so he must have died after that."

Either Marsden had come in the car with him and slipped out again, or Marsden had managed to get onto the base to lie in wait. Emily was sure it was Marsden who did this. Darryl had to be in this somehow. It was too much of a coincidence to die in this way with everything else going on.

This was too much for her right now. Emily didn't know what to think. She needed a few hours to herself to gather her thoughts into one place. To recharge. She swayed, Mike reached for her arm.

"You okay?"

"Yeah." Emily winced at the lie. "I'll be fine."

"We can talk about this in daylight when you're not looking ready to drop." Chambers looked around. "Are you going to a hotel tonight or are you staying?"

"I'm staying." That was in no question. "Mike's got someone to sort the front door out. I don't want to move around anymore than I have to."

Chambers looked like he was about to argue, but he opened and closed his mouth without any extra protest. He shook his head, pressing his fingers to the bridge of his nose.

"I know I won't be able to talk you out of it. It's far too late for that. Just stay here and don't leave the property until everything's sorted. Got it?"

"Got it."

Essentially, stay as a prisoner for a little longer. Emily didn't like the prospect. But at least she had decent company. Mike could keep her entertained.

She had to fight back a smile at that. Mike could keep her very entertained.

Chambers grunted. Then he turned towards the door.

"Just keep your head in this, Emily. Get some sleep and we'll talk tomorrow."

Get some sleep. That sounded like the best thing Chambers had said in a while.

Chapter Fifteen

B ut sleep wouldn't be entertained for some time. Emily had to give her statement to the cops. They treated her gently, although they did raise their eyebrows when Emily said she had been sleeping when the bomb went off. She didn't want to think what Mike had said in his own statement, but she was sticking to it.

It was close to two in the morning when the last truck pulled away. The crime scene team was finally finished and the bomb fragments had been taken back to the lab. Mike's friend had arrived with a brand new door and he and Mike were in the process of hanging it onto the front. Emily had started playing *Dead Space* again, just for something to keep her mind occupied while everything was going on, but she was so worn out she could barely keep her eyes open and her play was sluggish. Eventually, she turned off the TV and headed upstairs.

Instead of going to the spare room, she went into Mike's room. It felt like the most natural thing to do. Stripping down, Emily crawled naked into bed. This mattress was firmer than the one in the guest room, but it was comfortable. And it smelled of Mike, that subtle scent he wore on occasion. Emily burrowed down into the duvet and took a deep breath. The smell seemed to be very soothing. A bit like when her mother put lavender under her pillow as a child to help her sleep.

It certainly helped Emily. She closed her eyes and felt herself drifting off.

When Emily slowly roused herself from her sleep, she was aware of someone pressing against her back. An arm was around her waist, another body curled around hers, warm and solid. *Mike.* Emily sighed and shifted against him. It had been a long time since she had woken up in someone's arms. She could get used to this.

She felt Mike stir, his arm tightened around her. Then his hand slid up her belly and cupped her breast, circling her nipple with his finger. Emily felt her nipple harden under his delicate touch and she whimpered, which had Mike pinching her sensitive nub. His other hand snaked under her and palmed her other breast, pressing his very erect cock against her backside..

Emily reached back, curling her fingers around his shaft. Mike groaned and thrust into her hand.

"Emily, you feel so good." He started kissing her neck. "I should leave you to sleep, but I can't keep my hands off you."

"Then don't." Emily arched against him. "I think we were interrupted last night."

"Oh?" Mike's hand moved from her breast and trailed down her stomach, reaching between her legs. "You think we should carry on where we started?"

"Yes." Emily gasped as one finger dipped inside her pussy before withdrawing and tracing her clit. She wriggled against him, her hand tightening around his cock. "Please, Mike."

Mike didn't respond. He thrust his fingers into her pussy, his thumb pressed against her clit. Emily cried out, shuddering as he finger-fucked her at a fast pace that made the pleasure build at a rate that she wasn't used to. She writhed in Mike's arms, wanting to get close. She needed to get close. This felt so good.

One way to wake up in the morning.

Her orgasm made her break apart, heat making her body tingle. The feel of his fingers inside her, kneading her breast and his mouth at her neck was too much. Emily felt her orgasm crash down before building again. Mike was just relentless in wringing her out.

She was about to come again when Mike pulled his hands away. Emily was left hanging over the precipice and she tried to reach for him. Then Mike was getting up, rolling Emily onto her belly. He lifted her onto her hands and knees, nudging her legs apart as he pressed against her.

Then he thrust into her, almost catapulting Emily into the headboard.

Emily's orgasm exploded again, causing her to see bright lights behind her eyes. Mike was big, so much more than she thought. Her body stretched around him, tightening in a way that made Emily's orgasm ripple along.

Mike made a noise like a snarl.

"Hold onto the headboard." He commanded. "And don't move."

Don't move? How could she manage that?

Emily managed to reach up and got hold of the top of the headboard, which changed the angle of Mike's thrust. It felt deeper somehow. Sharper. Emily shuddered. Mike groaned, one hand gripping her hip as his other hand wound in her hair.

"Shit, Emily. I love how you feel around my cock."

He pulled out almost all the way and then slammed back in. His pace was hard, fast and deep. No slow, gentle ministrations, just fierce, intense fucking. Emily gripped onto the headboard to stop being thrown forward. It was difficult not to move when Mike was pounding into her like this, but she wasn't about to complain. This felt like she was flying, the pleasure building deep in her belly and spreading through her body, between her legs and up her spine. Another orgasm was coming, and this one was even stronger than the others.

How was this even possible?

Then all thoughts went out of her head as Mike, without slowing his thrusts, pulled her up against him, her back plastered against his chest. He let go of her hair and grasped her breast with one hand, pinching her nipple. His other hand went between her legs.

"Come for me again." He growled in her ear. "I want to feel you come around my cock."

Emily whimpered.

"I don't think I can."

"You can and you will." Mike tapped her clit. "Come for me, my sweet Emily."

Emily came. She screamed, reaching back and clutching hold of Mike's head as she tried to ride out the climax. It was too much. She couldn't take it. But Mike didn't let up, wrapping his arm across her chest as he increased his thrusts. He nuzzled her shoulder, and then bit down, which had Emily shrieking as another jolt of pleasure shot through her.

A moment later, Mike's cock twitched. He growled against her shoulder, and then his whole body shuddered as he came, his hold tightening around Emily he released inside her. Emily clutched onto him, unable to move. She felt like she was floating, not feeling in control of her body.

Mike was the first to move, easing them down onto the bed. He pulled out of her, which made Emily moan, and he rolled her onto her back before covering her with his body. Emily sank into his kiss, its sweetness a stark contrast to the way he had just taken her body. Mike was smiling as he broke the kiss.

"Morning."

"Morning." Emily managed to swallow back a yawn. "If it is morning."

"It's just gone seven." Mike stroked her cheek. "I was going to let you sleep, but I couldn't help myself."

Emily smiled, lifting a hand to stroke his jaw.

"Well, I could certainly get used to being woken up like that."

Something shifted in Mike's eyes. But then it was gone and he was smirking, walking his fingers up her belly and over her breastbone.

"I managed to complete my challenge. You came more than twice, I'm sure."

"Cocky bastard." Emily swatted his head. "Trust you to keep count."

"Well, you said you didn't have more than one orgasm." Mike nuzzled her cheek. "Proved you wrong."

"You are a cocky bastard." Emily couldn't help but laugh, arching her head back as he kissed down her neck. "But I won't be that loud if Prudence is home. I'm certainly not explaining that to her."

"You let me worry about that." Mike trailed kisses up her neck, finishing at her mouth. "You good to get up?"

"I think so." Emily frowned. "Will you let me go back to work? You told me that you would have my shift covered yesterday, but not for today."

Mike chuckled.

"You're that concerned about your job? You hate it."

"It's a force of habit." Emily tapped her fist to his shoulder. "And I shouldn't be getting privileges just becoming I'm fucking the boss."

"I don't know about that." Mike sighed. "You know, I made myself a rule never to have a relationship with any of my staff. You've just blown that out of the water."

"I didn't plan on doing it."

"I know that, but you've broken all my self-imposed rules." Mike kissed her gently. "I just don't know how I managed to keep my hands off you for so long."

Emily pressed her hands to his chest. She could feel his cock twitching against her thigh. He was getting hard again. How was he aroused again so soon?

"Just as long as you don't do it with all your staff."

"Jealous, are you?"

"I don't share."

Emily glanced away. She didn't even know what they had right now. But she knew that Mike was not going anywhere. She wouldn't share him with someone else.

Oh, Emily. You're such a goner.

"As it so happens, I'm taking a few days vacation as well. Callie can come and get the keys for the restaurant later." Mike pressed a kiss to her nose before he eased out of bed. "Right now, you and I need to get up and get to work."

"With what?"

"Finding out who else is on your list of suspects." Mike shot her a sly grin. "Fancy taking a shower together? Might be less time-consuming."

Emily laughed. No way was that going to be time-consuming. But she threw back the duvet and rose to her feet.

"As long as I get to wash your back first."

#

They took longer than they should have in the shower. The water was running cold by the time they got out, Emily practically shivering. Mike had been tempted to take her back to bed to warm her up, but then they would lose more time. He could do plenty of that later.

So much more later. Emily was addictive. Now Mike had touched her, felt her supple body and tasted her, he couldn't get enough. For the first time in years, he found himself with a stamina that he thought had disappeared when his wife died. Now Emily had walked into his life, bringing it all back to life.

Mike didn't want to see her walk back out again.

There was no discussion of a future, no suggestion that Emily was going to stay. She was a career soldier, through and through. Much like he had been when he was her age. That would be something she wouldn't give up so easily.

Would he be able to handle a long-distance relationship if they pursued one? Or would one of them be moving? Mike would do that if Emily was going back to her old base. It was where she was from, after all. Prudence was going off to college soon, and Mike could open up a business anywhere. As long as he had Emily in his life.

God, when did you become possessive over a woman?

Since the moment she walked into my life.

It was over an hour later before Mike and Emily were dressed and sitting at the kitchen table. Emily had on a white t-shirt and jeans, her hair done in a neat plait down her back. Mike would never figure out how women managed to do that. She gave him a smile and reached out to him.

"Good to go?"

"Yeah." Mike took her head, linking their fingers. "Good to go."

Emily smiled, and Mike felt warmth bloom in his chest. It made him want to lean over and kiss her. Instead, he cleared his throat and laid his cell phone on the table. They had agreed while dressing, keeping their distance from each other, that the best place to start would be looking over Marsden's original file. While he wasn't on base himself, Scott Warden could access it, and he had everything else they needed at his fingertips.

From the way Emily was, she was eager to get going. She looked a little lighter, a bit more color in her face and there was a sparkle in her eyes. Maybe it was because Marsden had been caught, the reason she had had to hide in the first place, or maybe it was because of their...activities.

Mike shoved those thoughts out of his head. Now was not the time to think how good Emily's mouth had felt around his cock in the shower. He dialled Scott's number and put it on loudspeaker, placing the cell phone on the table between them.

"Major Warden speaking."

"Hey, bud, it's me again."

"Mike! I heard what happened last night."

Emily raised her eyebrows. Mike frowned.

"How did you hear about it? You're nowhere near Union."

"You know that squaddies gossip and we're scattered all over the place. I've heard all about it since I got into the office this morning." Scott sniggered. "Dare I ask what you were doing when Marsden tried to get in? Because from what I've heard, you were rather...busy when he turned up."

Mike cleared his throat.

"Scott, I'm not alone. I have Lieutenant Emily O'Rourke here with me. We wanted to ask you if you could dig out Marsden's file for us."

"Oh. I see." Scott coughed. "Sorry, I forgot we were in mixed company."

"Rib him about whatever he might have done later, Major Warden." Emily leaned forward. She was back into her cool, soldier mode. That should not be so arousing. "Marsden's case file and trial were all put into the system. You should be able to access it through my account."

"Right. Okay." Mike could hear the smirk in his friend's voice. "Give me your access details and I'll get into it."

Emily gave him the details, and there was the sound of tapping at Scott's end. A few moments later, after a lot of humming, Scott came back on the line.

"Okay, I've got it. What are you looking for?"

Emily glanced at Mike, who nodded.

"We think Marsden had a partner in all this. Someone had to have got him out of prison and then help him murder Karen and Susan."

"You think someone involved immediately in the trial was a partner?"

"Or someone close to him. We want to know where everyone who was prominently involved in the trial checked to see where they are, alibis, the lot. Once they're all crossed off the list, we'll cast the net wider."

"An inside man. Or woman." Scott whistled. "When I heard about this case last year, I thought it was cut and dry."

"The case was cut and dry. Dealing with a misogynistic psychopath was something else entirely." Emily rubbed at her eyes. "I would love to get back to a normal life without having to look over my shoulders."

"Understood. Does your commanding officer know that you're doing this?"

"I plead the fifth on that."

Mike bit back a smile. Scott chuckled.

"From what I've heard of your reputation, Lieutenant, that doesn't surprise me. I can get all the names listed on here and check them out, not a problem. Do any of the people involved jump out at you as potential suspects?"

Emily bit her lip.

"Not really. But after three deaths already, I want to largely make sure they're all okay."

Three? Then Mike remembered. Samir Kashefi. Emily had told him about that earlier. Three men from Marsden's trial were dead, and a fourth was targeted. It wouldn't be too much of a stretch to think everyone else had a target painted on their back.

"Can you also ask your social worker friend to get hold of Marsden's records when he was in the care system?" Mike asked. "I seem to remember he made a big stink about being a foster kid in the trial transcripts." He glanced at Emily for confirmation and she nodded. "Maybe we could find family that way, if he connected with relatives from his birth family."

"I'll see what I can do, but I can't promise anything. That could take a while."

"We can wait."

"I'm sure." There was a tapping of keys, and then Scott's voice returned. "You say that Karen Underwood, Samir Kashefi and Susan Grey are dead?"

"Yes?"

"Well, you can add another to your list. Jorge Rodriguez."

Mike frowned at Emily, whose eyes had widened.

"He was one of the court officers. A ruthless man when needed to be but a real sweetheart out of it. He's dead as well?"

"I'm afraid so. I thought his name sounded familiar, so I did a quick search." Scott sounded grim. "He had just moved to Seattle for a new job and then had a heart attack in his apartment."

Emily looked like she had seen a ghost. Mike thought she was about to faint.

"But…Jorge was only thirty. He was very healthy."

"That's what the official cause of death was. It's going to take a lot of favors to get that autopsy report."

Mike waited for Emily to answer, but she didn't reply. Instead, she rose and walked towards the newly mended back door, wrapping her arms around her middle. She seemed to be closing herself off again.

"Hello? Anyone there?"

"I'm here, Scott." Mike turned back to his phone. "Just see what you can do. We've already had three murdered and Marsden's actively tried to kill Emily. Rodriguez was involved, so we need to check."

"On it." Scott sighed. "You know, maybe I should retire from the army and become a private detective. That's all you seem to be using me for right now."

"That's because you're damned good at getting blood out of a stone." Mike glanced at Emily, but she didn't turn around. "We want to account for the judge, the defence team, the jury if there was one, court ushers, security guards, the lot. Chambers made sure everyone cut contact with Emily to keep her safe, so none of them would have known where she was."

"So, the only person who knew was Colonel Chambers." Scott paused. "Do you think he could be the partner?"

"No." Mike looked up at Emily. She didn't turn around as she spoke. "Kenneth Chambers can be an ass at times, but his loyalty has never been brought into question. I don't believe he would do that."

Mike believed her. His gut said that Chambers was a damn good soldier and it was his whole life. And there was a certain fondness for Emily that showed whenever he looked at her. Mike had seen it several times. Chambers cared for Emily. He wouldn't hurt her.

"Besides, with Chambers running around getting things sorted with Marsden to transport him to jail after surgery, he's going to be limited in his findings." Mike grinned. "What he can find out in a day you can find out in five seconds."

"I'm flattered." Scott drawled. "You can stop buttering me up, you know."

"Where's the fun in that?"

Scott made a groaning sound. Mike was sure he was rolling his eyes.

"Okay, fine, I'll see what I can do. I don't get paid enough for this."

"You love me, really."

"Don't get me started, Michael."

Mike chuckled.

"Thanks, Scott. I'll check in later."

He hung up. Then he turned to Emily, who had opened the door and stepped out onto the back porch. Rising to his feet, Mike followed her. Emily stood on the edge of the wooden porch, staring out over his back yard.

"Emily?"

Emily didn't answer. Mike reached out and touched her back.

"Honey?"

"What have I started, Mike?"

Her composure had slipped. Mike wrapped his arms around her, tugging her to lean back against him. Emily sighed and rested her head on his shoulder.

"You make it sound like this was all your fault."

"There are moments when I feel like it is." Emily closed her eyes. "I'm just so tired of this."

"I know you are." Mike kissed her temple. "And remember, none of this is your fault. The one at fault is Marsden for even thinking he could deal with the enemy. He committed a crime and you were doing your job. The fact he got pissed and came after you has nothing to do with it being your fault. That's on him."

"I know that. It doesn't make me feel any better." Emily rested her hand on his arm, a slight smile drifting across her mouth. "But having you around

136

when this first happened would have helped."

Mike's chest tightened at that. He gently grasped her chin and turned her head, pressing a soft kiss to her lips.

"I'm here now. And I'm not going anywhere."

Chapter Sixteen

"Are you not?"

Emily opened her eyes. Mike's face was so close to hers. She felt his smile brush across her mouth.

"No, I'm not. You want me around? Then I'm staying. Besides," his hand came up and gently palmed her breast, "the benefits of sticking around are certainly swaying my opinion."

Emily wanted to retort, but the shot of lust that hit her left her speechless as Mike squeezed her breast. She didn't think it was possible to switch it on so quickly. After the shock knowing Jorge was dead, Emily hadn't thought she could be so aroused. Mike was just making all new rules, and Emily was struggling to keep up. She whimpered as Mike's other hand slid under her t-shirt.

"Mike…"

"Just say the word, Emily, and I won't go anywhere." His fingers dipped under her waistband as he kissed her. "Just say yes."

How could she deny him something like that? Emily turned in his arms, cupping his face in her hands.

"Yes."

Mike growled. He grabbed her and hauled her against his chest as he kissed her hard enough to make her breathless. Emily wrapped her arms around his neck and held on, sure that her legs were going to give way.

Mike lifted her off her feet, wrapping her legs around his waist. When he broke the kiss, Mike was panting.

"We seem to be getting into this position a lot, don't we?"

"What can I say?" Emily rolled her hips against his erection, eliciting a moan from both of them. "I love having someone taking charge."

"I noticed." Mike nipped at her jaw with his teeth before kissing her neck. "Maybe we should make the most of this position. I know it can be…exciting."

Emily shivered, gasping as Mike sucked at the skin where her neck met her shoulder.

"Sounds like an idea. But…shouldn't we be doing some work?"

"That can come later." Mike's growl vibrated through her body. "I think we've got something more…pressing to deal with."

Emily held on as he strode into the house. They were halfway across the kitchen when the doorbell rang. Mike froze, and Emily's lust dissipated in a puff of smoke. Mike eased her down to the floor, shifting her to one side.

"Stay here." He murmured. "I'll go and see who it is."

"It's probably just the cops. Or it could be Colonel Chambers."

Mike grunted. He picked up his gun from the table and took the safety off. "Just in case. Back me up just in case?"

"Sure." Emily picked up the other gun and turned to him. "Always."

Mike stared at her. Then he grasped her chin and kissed her hard.

"That's a promise for later."

Stepping back, he headed into the hall. Emily hovered just out of sight as the doorbell went again. It could just be an innocent caller, or it could be Marsden's associate drawing them out. It had happened before in Emily's experience.

Not that Mike would pay any attention.

"Who is it?"

"It's Callie, Mike." Emily relaxed when she heard a familiar voice. "You said you couldn't get to the restaurant and could I open the place up?"

"Oh, right. Hang on."

A moment later, Mike appeared back in the kitchen. Emily frowned as she realized something.

"Hang on, if you were with me, who opened up yesterday?"

"I did." Mike started checking each counter. "You were fast asleep and the alarm was on. Things were secure enough, so I thought you would be safe."

He made a face. "I'm just glad Marsden didn't try anything while I wasn't here."

"I see." Emily folded her arms. "Nice to know you cared."

"Don't start. You can argue with me about that later." Retrieving the keys from beside the bread bin, Mike went back to the door. "I'm sure you can figure out how to make me pay."

Flashing her a wink, Mike disappeared into the hallway. Moments later, Emily heard him opening the door and there was a jangling of keys.

"Here. Thanks for this, Callie. Things are a little hectic at the moment."

"I'll say." There was a hint of amusement in Callie's voice. "I heard a rumour around the restaurant about Emily. Something about you two calling in sick at the same time. There's a lot of speculation about what's going on."

Emily bit back a groan. So much for people not knowing where she was. If Marsden had heard the rumours, he would have put two and two together. They wouldn't have needed to be followed if he was listening to waitresses gossiping.

"I'm sure I've told you before about gossiping, Callie." Mike's voice had sharpened. Callie laughed.

"I wasn't gossiping, I'm just letting you know. I thought that was a line you wouldn't cross."

"That will be all, Callie. And if anything happens, you know how to get hold of me."

Callie was still laughing as she walked away. Moments later, the door closed. Emily put her gun down and moved into the doorway. Mike was standing in the hall, running his hand over his face.

"Now everyone knows where I am." Emily grunted. "Great. Just great."

Mike looked at her.

"That doesn't mean you're moving, are you?"

"No, I'm not going anywhere." Emily approached him, plucking the gun from his hand and putting it on the hall table. "But I think this might mean I'll need another job."

"I thought you were going to go back to your hometown once this was over."

"I haven't decided yet." Emily smiled as she pressed her hands against his chest. "Maybe if I have an incentive to stay...I'm sure I can reconsider my position."

Mike's eyes seemed to glow red-hot. His hands rested on her hips.

"How do you want this incentive? I'm sure I can think of something."

"I've got a few ways." Emily reached up on her toes, brushing her mouth over his. "Come with me. And you do as I say for once."

"I think I can manage that." Mike growled as he took Emily's hand and pressed it to his erection. "Just tell me what you want."

"You, naked, on the couch." Emily drew back and rubbed at Mike's erection before stepping back. "Think you can do that?"

"You not going to undress me?"

"You do as I say, Sergeant."

Mike's nostrils flared. Then he took her hand and led her into the living room. Pressing a kiss to her knuckles, Mike undressed, kicking his clothes aside before sitting on the couch with his legs spread. His cock stood erect, pre-cum at the tip. Emily's mouth went dry as she took him in. He was magnificent for his age. Every inch of him was built and toned. Emily wanted to spend the day licking every part of his body.

"You keep looking at me like that, Emily," Mike touched his cock and started to stroke himself, "and I'm not going to last very long."

"Can't have that, can we?" Emily reached for her t-shirt. "And don't touch your cock. That's just for me."

"Yes, ma'am." Mike pulled his hand away, putting both hands behind his head. "Are you this bossy when you're at work?"

"Maybe." Emily slowly lifted her shirt, revealing her belly inch by inch. "You have to be bossy to get where I am."

"I don't doubt it."

Mike's eyes glowed as Emily began to undress. She moved very slowly, teasing him as she divested each item of clothing. Mike growled as she delicately tugged her jeans down, bending at the hip as she lowered them to the floor.

"You are such a tease. I swear you've been teasing me for months."

"I was going to say the same about you." Emily straightened up and stepped out of her jeans. "I wanted to throttle Chambers for putting me with you."

"Oh? You think I was teasing you?"

"You must've been." Emily ran her hands over her breasts and down her belly. "You made me feel hot all over. Especially here."

She cupped herself and watched as Mike's eyes followed her hand. So much for teasing him; she had just made herself even hungrier for him. Slipping her panties off, Emily kicked them aside.

"I think I'm done teasing." She got on the couch, straddling his hips. "I thought I could, but you're just too much."

"That a good or a bad thing?"

Emily reached between them, grasping Mike's cock. Mike hissed, his hands gripping at her hips.

"Depends on if you wanted this to last longer." Emily panted as she rubbed her pussy over his cock. He felt even wider like this, and Emily had to stop to get her breath. Wow.

"We can prolong it later." Mike's hands tightened on her hips. "Right now, just ride me."

"I thought I was in charge."

"Not anymore."

Mike slammed her down onto his cock. Emily moaned, her whole body burning up as she adjusted to his size. White light flashed before her eyes, and she found herself shaking. She was so close to coming and she hadn't even started yet.

"Fuck, Emily," Mike started to urge her to move. "Ride me. I want to see you."

Emily couldn't fight him. She didn't want to. She started to ride his cock, each thrust inside her making the pleasure ripple all through her body and build higher and higher. Mike held onto her and met her thrusts with his own. He pulled her down, taking her breast into his mouth as he squeezed her butt cheeks. The sensation of his hands on her, his mouth devouring her breast and his cock inside her, had her pleasure twisting inside her. Emily could hardly breathe. She bit down on Mike's shoulder, which had Mike biting down on her breast in response.

Her ograsm exploded, and for a moment everything went black. Emily was aware of her screaming Mike's name, gripping onto his shoulders as he pounded into her, her body shaking too much to meet his thrusts. Then Mike pressed her hips down hard with a snarl of his own as he came, his cock twitching hard with his release. Emily could feel his heartbeat racing against her chest. Or was it hers? She wasn't sure anymore.

She just knew as Mike cradled her head as he kissed her that she had got past the point of caring.

#

The sound of his cell phone ringing roused Mike from his sleep. It took him a moment for him to realize where he was. In his bed, with Emily curled into his side as she slept, her head on his chest with her hand on his belly. At some point, they had managed to get up to the bedroom to carry on what happened downstairs.

So much for doing their own investigation. But Mike liked to think they made use of their time. And he liked waking up like this. He could get used to this again.

Answer the phone, you idiot.

Rolling over, Mike reached for his cell phone. The time said it was ten-thirty at night. Mike couldn't remember the last time he had spent the day in bed with a woman. Probably the first day Prudence went to school. That had been a good day.

Emily stirred as Mike fumbled to answer the call.

"What? What's that?"

"It's Scott. He's probably got something for us."

Emily rolled on her back and yawned, rubbing at her eyes.

"Let's see what he has to say. I'm sure he's been more productive than we have."

"You mean what we've done all day hasn't been productive?"

Emily stuck her tongue out at him.

"You know what I mean."

"I do." Mike rolled over and kissed her before sitting up. "And I'll make sure you're kept productive later."

Emily purred and stretched her arms above her head. The duvet had slipped off her to her waist, and Mike couldn't take his eyes off her breasts.

"I'll look forward to that. But you'd better answer the call first."

"What? Oh." Mike sat cross-legged on the bed and pressed to answer. "Hey, Scott."

"Interrupting something, was I?"

"I was asleep."

"I see." Scott's voice was laced with amusement. "I'm sure you weren't sleeping alone."

"Sharp, isn't he?" Emily drawled.

Mike groaned as Scott burst out laughing.

"Nice to see you've got some energy left in you, Mike."

"Fuck you."

"No, thanks. Not my type. And I'm sure Lieutenant O'Rourke might object to sharing you."

"I don't know about that." Emily sat up with a large grin. "Are you as handsome as Mike?"

"I object to sharing." Mike warned. "What have you got for us, Scott? I'm sure you didn't call to discuss an orgy."

"Oh, I'd love to, but I do have news. I've managed to find most of the names of those involved in the trial."

Mike saw Emily sitting up. That was something.

"Who haven't you found yet?"

"I'm still going through all the jurors and checking the court officials who would've been in the room. But the jurors I have found are still alive and well. Lieutenant O'Rourke's team is okay. Ben McGrath and Sean Carey are still on base. Lee Morris is now stationed in Germany and Evie Mateou is visiting her mother in Nova Scotia while she goes through chemo."

That was something, and Mike saw Emily's shoulders slump in relief.

"Has there been any attempt on their lives?"

"No. I spoke to each of them, and there was nothing. But McGrath and Carey have homes on-base, Morris is on another continent and Mateou's mother's home is in the middle of nowhere with limited ways to reach it. Marsden only managed to get to O'Rourke because her house was off-base."

"Reminds me to go house-hunting when this is done." Emily muttered.

That had Mike's chest tightening. House-hunting. Did that mean she was still leaving?

"What about the court side of it?" Mike asked. "Underwood and Kashefi were in the army. What about the defence team?"

"They were civilians. I think one of Marsden's 'associates' recommended them." Scott's voice turned grim. "They're dead as well."

Emily's eyes widened.

"What?"

"Jason Yip was the lead. He was found tortured in his home by his wife. Second chair Daniel Trudge was killed in a drive-by shooting. Because of the people they represented, most of whom were involved in organized crime, nobody made the connection."

"Holy shit." Emily breathed.

Mike agreed with the sentiment.

"When were they killed?" He asked.

"Yip was killed about a week after O'Rourke disappeared. Trudge was four days later."

That sounded like Marsden got pissed that Emily had vanished without a trace and took his anger out on his defence team. From what Emily had told Mike about the case in between love-making, his defence team were ruthless and tried many underhanded tactics until the judge told them to cut it out. It didn't make a difference; Marsden still got twenty years in jail.

It was certainly going to be a lot longer now once he was connected to these murders.

"What about the Judge?" Emily asked. "Judge Wardle?"

Scott sighed.

"Judge Lewis Wardle is still alive, but he's paralysed. He was attacked in his house three months ago. He fought back, but was shot in the spine. He'll never walk again."

Emily put her hand over her mouth. Mike could see the pain there. He reached out and took her hand, kissing her fingers. Emily took a deep breath and lowered her hand, squeezing his hand with a slight smile.

"Mike? You there?"

"I'm still here."

"I've got something else. I managed to get access to the court records and prison logs from a friend who works in the prison system. I owe him a couple of season tickets to the baseball as a result, but it was worth it."

"What is it?"

"I noticed that Marsden was visited in prison on a very regular basis by one person. She put down that she was his lawyer in the sign-in sheets."

"Which means attorney-client privilege and no cameras to record their visit." Emily murmured. "We didn't know about another girlfriend."

"We don't know who she is other than a name. Things are a bit sketchy right now." There was a rustling of papers on Scott's end. "She's not listed on the bar, but she did come up as an employee in Yip's law firm as a filing clerk. Her name is Shelley Barton."

Just what they needed. A groupie. Mike had heard of these people who would become obsessed with dangerous men to the point they declared their undying love. He had never seen the fascination or even pretended to understand the mentality.

"Where is she now, Scott?"

"No idea. I'm still looking."

"You can find anyone."

"Within my limits, and I've stretched my favors to those limits." Scott said grimly. "Shelley Barton has completely fallen off the grid. She disappeared shortly before Marsden broke out of jail."

Was she another victim? Or another co-conspirator? Mike rubbed at his eyes.

"Thanks, Scott. Let us know if you do find anything on her."

"I'm using my last favor to pull up her file. If I push it any further, I'm going to get into trouble."

"I'll take the blame for that. You've gone above and beyond what a friend would do."

"I'll remember that." Scott chuckled. "Maybe you should give me the money for those season tickets."

Emily giggled. Mike had to smile.

"I'll see what I can do. Thanks again."

He hung up, tossing his cell phone onto the bedside table. Emily rubbed at her temples.

"Shelley Barton. The name doesn't ring a bell. I didn't come into much contact with the defence team if I could help it. I certainly wouldn't have come into contact with the filing clerks."

"Well, I'm sure we're going to figure that out." Mike looked away. "Could you sit in a different position, Emily?"

"Why?"

"It's a little distracting."

Sitting as she was, her pussy was on display. And Mike could feel his exhausted body stirring again. Emily arched an eyebrow, a smirk twitching at her mouth.

"Oh? It's distracting, is it?" She spread her legs and sat back on her hands. "How about now?"

Mike groaned. Damn, she was a tease. He crawled over, pinning Emily to the bed.

"You are insatiable, Lieutenant." He whispered, dipping his fingers into her pussy before brushing over her clit.

"I was going to say the same about you." Emily sighed as she arched her back. "You just make me want you more."

"You're not tired." Mike watched as Emily winched when his fingers stroked her lips. "You must be sore."

"Not for everything." Emily cupped his jaw in her hands. "Just don't stop touching me, Mike."

How could he deny something like that? Mike bent his head and started kissing her neck, licking a line up to her jaw before kissing her ear.

"I'm sure I'm going to have a heart attack if you kept me going." He whispered, kissing her cheek, across to her nose, and then her mouth. "I won't be able to keep up soon."

"I was going to say the same thing about you."

"I'm much older than you, Emily."

Emily kissed her, lifting her hips against his hand.

"You're not old. You're…you're you."

Her kiss was sweet, delicate. Mike closed his eyes and savored it. God, he could make love to her all night and not get bored. Exhausted, yes, but not bored. This could be something he could easily get used to.

If he could persuade Emily to stay. If she went back, he would be going with her. But Mike would prefer that Emily stayed with him. Where she belonged.

His phone started ringing again as he started to shift down her body. Emily groaned.

"Dammit. Perfect timing again."

"Ignore it." Mike flicked his tongue over her nipple. "They'll call back."

"It could be Callie. Something could be wrong at work."

She was right. Mike growled and rose up, pressing a hard kiss to her mouth before rolling away. It was a number he didn't recognize. Nevertheless, he answered it. The quicker he answered, the quicker he could go back to burying himself in the gorgeous woman in his bed.

"Wilson."

"Wilson, it's Detective Winston."

It was the solemn tone of the man's voice that had all thoughts of sex leave Mike in a rush. He sat up.

"What's wrong?"

"It's your daughter. She's in the hospital."

The world seemed to stop. Prudence was in hospital? Emily shifted behind him, wrapping her arms around his shoulders.

"Mike?"

"What happened, Winson?"

"She's not badly hurt, but she's shaken up. She asked if I could call you."

"Union Hospital?"

"Yes."

"I'm on my way now."

Mike hung up, staring at his cell. Prudence was hurt. And he was frozen.

"Mike?" Emily gently shook his shoulders. "What's happened?"

"Prudence is in hospital. She's been attacked."

Emily was silent for a split second. Then she was jumping off the bed and hurrying to Mike's dresser.

"Get dressed." She pulled out some clothes and tossed them at him. "I'll get some clothes on and call a taxi."

"You're coming with me?"

"Of course." Emily shook her head. "You don't think I'm going to leave you now, are you? You need someone with you, whether you like it or not. And I'm going with you to make sure your daughter is in one piece."

Mike didn't know what to say to that. If he did, he was sure he was going to break down.

Chapter Seventeen

Prudence was hurt. Mike's heart was racing as he and Emily ran into the hospital. Someone had jumped her as she left her friend's house. All Winston would say was that she had been taken to the ER.

Damn that man. He needed more details. His daughter had been attacked. Mike's mind was turning over everything that could have happened. Had she been shot? Stabbed? Strangled? He had no idea. All he knew was he wouldn't be able to calm down until he had seen her. Heard her speak. Then Mike would know she was okay.

The ER was packed. People were milling around everywhere, both patients and staff. Just the knowledge that he was going to be shoved into a tightly confined space with a crowd of people had Mike's chest tightening in panic. Working a restaurant was one thing; he could stay behind the bar or escape to his office if it got too much for him. This? It was going to be hell.

Emily eased in against his side as he stood at the edge of the ER and took his hand.

"I'm here." She murmured. "I'm not going anywhere."

Mike squeezed her hand in return. Just having her close by was calming enough. Keeping hold of her hand, they headed through the throng of people. It looked like a big accident had occurred in the last hour and each of the rooms seemed jam-packed.

They found Prudence in the end cubicle. Winston was with her, sitting on her bed. He rose to his feet as Mike stepped through the curtains. Prudence sat up.

"Dad!"

Mike hurried over, hugging Prudence tightly as she wrapped her arms around his neck. She gave a small sob, burying her face into his sweater. Mike wasn't sure which one of them was trembling the most. He eased her back and cupped her head in his hands. She was pale, and there was a bruise coming up under her eye, but she didn't look any worse for wear.

"How bad were you hurt?"

"Not much." Prudence bit her lip. "Someone...someone jumped me as I left my friend Sophie's house. They put something around my neck and they started to pull." She touched her neck, and Mike saw the red welts around her throat. "I fought back, got my gun out and clobbered them one. Caught them in the face."

"Good girl." Mike stroked her cheek. "Next time you can pull the trigger, okay?"

"I'm not a soldier, Dad. It's not an instinctive reaction." Prudence gulped and then flinched. "Damn, that hurts."

"Take it easy, honey." Mike kissed her forehead. He turned to Winston. "What happened to the bastard who did this?"

"Whoever it was had vanished before we got there. Prudence..." Winston cleared his throat. "Miss Wilson was being seen by her friend. She had passed out after hitting her head."

"You hit your head?" Mike glared at his daughter. "When were you going to tell me about that?"

"Dad, I'm alive! I'm okay!" Prudence began to tremble. "Please don't start shouting at me. Detective Winston has only just calmed me down."

She looked close to tears. Mike swallowed and fought down his anger. Someone had gone after his daughter, and they had got away. It had to be Barton. She had to be targeting Prudence because of her link to Emily.

To him. Was he a target now?

"Mike."

A hand rested on his back as he heard Emily's voice. And just like that, the tension seemed to ease. The anger was still there, but it was pulling back. Mike didn't have the need to pick up something and throw it.

"I...I'll give you a few moments." Winston headed towards the curtains. "I still need to take Miss Wilson's statement."

He disappeared outside, shutting the curtains behind him. Mike turned to Prudence, stroking her hair away from her forehead.

"How's the head?"

"Sore, but I'll live." Prudence managed a small smile. "Thank you."

"For what?"

"Not getting mad. I could see you wanted to."

"I still want to." Mike kissed her forehead. "I should've been there. You shouldn't have been out alone."

"Dad, we didn't know I was going to get jumped. And after what you told me happened last night, do you really think I should've been at home?"

She did have a point. Mike couldn't guarantee that Prudence would be safe had the bomb gone off. Then he recalled what he and Emily had been up to, and he was glad that she hadn't been there. Neither of them had been exactly quiet.

"Dad?"

"Hmm?"

"You're going red." Prudence raised her eyebrows. "You okay?"

"Oh. Right. I'm fine." Mike straightened up. "I'm just going to speak to Detective Winston. Emily will stay here with you. That good with you?"

"Sure."

Prudence was still giving him a quizzical look. Mike knew she would be asking a lot of questions later. He turned to Emily.

"Stay with her. And don't go anywhere unless I'm with you."

Emily frowned.

"I'm not completely helpless, you know."

"It would make me feel better if you stayed in one place." Mike cupped her jaw in his palm. "Please, Emily? After what's happened, I need to know you and my daughter are safe."

Emily looked like she was about to argue, but she didn't. Wise move. Mike was not about to go into it with her in front of his kid. The two people he loved had been hurt, and he didn't want that to happen again.

Love. He did love her.

"Okay, fine." Emily pouted. "But we're going to be talking about your commands when we get out in the open, Mike."

"Oh, I'm sure we will." Not caring that his daughter could see them, Mike gave Emily a kiss that left her gasping when he pulled away. "Be good."

He was aware of Prudence giggling as he left the cubicle. And Mike couldn't stop himself from smiling. Winston looked at him strangely.

"What was that about?"

"Don't ask. You're too young to know." Mike gestured towards the fire escape. "We're going to go somewhere quiet, Detective. I think we've got a lot to discuss."

#

"So, what's going on with you and Dad?"

Prudence had a sly grin on her face. Emily cleared her throat, but couldn't stop herself from smiling.

"I think you're a little too young to know what's going on."

"Come on! I'm not a little girl!"

"And do you really want to know the ins and outs of what your dad does?"

Prudence's mouth opened and closed. Then she made a face.

"I suppose you're right. Maybe I don't want to know." She shuddered. "God, that would give me nightmares."

"Cheeky madam." Emily sat on the edge of the bed. "How are you holding up?"

"Better now Dad's here."

"You know he feels guilty about what happened."

Prudence shook her head.

"It's not his fault."

No. It's mine. But Emily kept quiet.

"He's your father. When you're a parent, it's difficult to switch any emotions off when their kid has been hurt."

"I've got a hard head. I'll live." Prudence flexed her hand, and Emily noticed the swollen knuckles. "I caught them with the gun, as did my knuckles. They're going to be walking around with an impressive black eye."

Emily hoped so. At least it might make it easier to find Marsden's partner.

She was under no illusions that it was someone other than Shelley Barton who had been helping Marsden go after everyone in his trial. She had to have gone after Prudence herself. But to what end? Draw Mike out so Emily would come after him? It was possible.

But to bring an eighteen-year-old kid into this mess? That was a line Emily would not cross. And Barton would have figured that out for herself after grappling with Prudence Wilson.

"Emily?"

"What?"

Emily blinked. Prudence smiled.

"You wandered off there."

"Oh. Sorry."

Prudence sat forward and squeezed Emily's arm.

"I said I'm going to be okay. Dad will be as well. We're tougher than we make out to be."

"I've noticed that about your dad."

Prudence grinned.

"He's a good guy. Rough around the edges, and a bit of a control freak, but he's a good guy under all that."

"I know that already." Emily smiled. "I've known it for some time."

"And he loves you."

"What?" Emily started. "What makes you say that?"

"The way he was around you just now. Dad's not a touchy-feely guy, not even with that bitch Carol. And he kissed you in front of me like he was starving." Prudence shrugged. "I may be young, but I know my father. You're someone special to him."

Someone special to him. Emily could certainly hope for that. Maybe if she had an inkling, an indication, that Mike wanted her around then she would see about staying in Union. There was no point staying if there wasn't anything - or anyone - to keep her there.

From what Prudence had just said, there was plenty of reason now to stay.

Emily jumped when something started buzzing. For a moment, she had no idea what it was. Prudence raised her eyebrows.

"That's your cell phone, Emily."

"What? Oh, right."

Emily fumbled in her pockets, almost dropping her phone as she finally retrieved it. It was Callie. Why was she calling her? Was something wrong at the restaurant? Emily answered before it went to voicemail.

"Callie, you okay?"

"Oh, Molly! Thank God!"

It took a moment for Emily to remember that Callie was addressing her. Molly Ferrel felt like a lifetime ago. Then Emily sat up. Callie sounded like she was in hysterics, barely holding back sobbing. What had happened between her leaving Mike's place and now? Had Barton found her as well?

"Callie? What is it? I can't understand you."

"I...I don't know what to do." Callie was breathing heavily, her voice shaking. "Someone just came into the bar and threatened me. Said if I didn't tell him where you were, he was...he was going to burn the place down!"

Emily stared at her phone as Callie started sobbing again. A man had come in and threatened her? Was this Barton's doing? And why would Barton threaten Callie? She was just an employee, barely any connection to Emily except they worked together. There wasn't much leverage there.

Was there?

"I need you to come here, Molly." Callie whimpered. "Quickly. I'm scared. Everyone else has gone home and I'm nervous about leaving on my own."

"I need to tell Mike about this." Emily said. "He's the boss. If someone's threatening his business..."

"I've already called him. He said I needed to call the cops and sit tight, but I don't want to be alone." Callie gave out another sob. "Please, Molly?"

Emily was torn. Mike had told her to stay with Prudence, not to go anywhere. But Callie was in trouble, and she needed someone there. Emily was not someone who backed away from helping a friend.

Mike would understand.

"Okay. I'll make my way over now. Just sit tight until I get there. Have you called the cops?"

"Not yet."

"Then do it. I'll be right over."

Emily hung up and shifted off the bed. Prudence was frowning at her.

"Are you serious? Dad said you had to stay here."

"He'll be along once he's dealt with Detective Winston. Callie needs me now." Emily squeezed Prudence's hand. "I'll be right back once I know she's okay."

Prudence frowned.

"Dad's going to be pissed that you left."

"Then he can yell at me later." Emily stepped out of the cubicle. "Sit tight. I'll be back soon."

Chapter Eighteen

Emily felt her cell phone buzzing again and slid her hand into her pocket to hang up. It was more than likely going to be Mike again. He must have realized she was gone.

He was going to be pissed. But Emily didn't want him to leave Prudence's side. She needed her dad more than Emily needed him. And Emily wasn't going unarmed; her gun was in its holster under her jacket and her backup was strapped in a hidden pocket on the back of her jacket. Even though this was Callie, Emily wasn't going in without some kind of backup.

The taxi pulled up outside the restaurant and Emily jumped out, barely stopping to shove a handful of bills into the driver's hand. The restaurant looked dark, no sign of life at all. Emily tried the front door, but it was locked. She jogged around the back, and saw the back door open. On the alert, Emily took out her gun and slowed her pace.

This could be Callie leaving her a way in. Or someone else could have come in. Maybe the guy had come back and had Callie. Maybe...

Calm down, your mind's racing. Focus.

Emily was almost at the door when a shadow appeared in the doorway. A second later, Callie was stepping outside. She looked like she was about to cry, practically shaking as she hurried to Emily.

"Thank God you're here, Emily!" She stumbled, and Emily caught her before she hit the ground. "I thought it was him coming back."

"Calm down, Callie." Emily tucked her gun into the back of her jeans. Callie was leaning into her so much that she couldn't holster. She set the other woman back on her feet. "Tell me what happened."

"Well, everyone else had gone." Callie's hand was trembling as she brushed her hair out of her eyes. "I was locking up when someone approached me. He…he demanded to know where you were. I said I didn't know, and he threatened me." She touched her cheek and winced. "He punched me and told me that he would come back to burn the place down if he didn't get the answers he wanted from me. I…I didn't know what to do."

Someone had come to the restaurant and threatened Callie? That didn't make any sense. If it was Marsden's co-conspirator, why would they go after Callie? But Callie was clearly terrified, and Emily wasn't about to question her.

"Okay, let's get back inside." She led Callie back to the fire escape. "Have you called the cops?"

"They're on their way." Callie whimpered. "It feels like they're taking forever."

"They will be here." Emily urged her into the locker room. "Let's go to Mike's office and have a look at the CCTV footage. We'll have caught it all on tape."

"Okay."

Stepping around her, Emily headed through the restaurant and into the stairwell to Mike's office. If whoever it was came here, they would have been caught on camera. Mika kept security cameras on everything, saying that it was better to be safe than sorry. After seeing how he had equipped both his home and his business, Emily was glad of it. If it hadn't been there…

She wasn't going to think about it. Not now.

Emily was halfway up the stairs when she realized that Callie wasn't following her. The manager had disappeared. She was just behind her. Confused, Emily went back down the stairs.

"Callie? Callie, are you there?"

She stepped into the main restaurant. It was pitch black and quiet. There was no sign of Callie anywhere.

Where had she gone?

Wait a minute. She called you Emily.

There was a shuffling behind her. Emily turned, hand going for her gun, and then something slammed into her head. Pain exploded in her face, and then everything went black.

#

Mike was torn beginning fuming and panicking. Emily shouldn't have gone off on her own. She had said she would stay with Prudence, but moments after he walked away Emily had disappeared. It didn't matter if Callie wanted her help on something, she shouldn't have gone anywhere.

And that was another thing. Callie had claimed to have tried to get hold of him. But Mike had no record of Callie calling him. Was she forced to make the call to draw Callie out? Or was there something else going on?

Mike's hands were shaking as he made a phone call, getting a car to the hospital as quickly as possible. He needed to get over to his restaurant fast, but he couldn't leave Prudence alone. His daughter may have been protesting that she was okay on her own, but Mike wasn't about to walk out with her unprotected. Winston had stepped in saying he would keep an eye on her, claiming he needed to take a statement. From the way he was hovering around Prudence, Mike suspected something else was making him stay. But he was too worried about Emily to think too much about it. That would come later.

Mike hurried out to the parking lot, trying Emily again. She wasn't answering his calls. She hung up the last two. What was she playing at? Her life had been in danger for months, and she had been attacked twice in three days. What part of that said it was a good idea to go out on her own?

She deserved a spanking for that.

He was pacing around the parking lot when a car pulled up beside him with a screeching of tyres. Chambers leaned over and opened the passenger door.

"Get in."

Mike jumped in, barely shutting the door before the colonel pulled away. He gripped onto his seat as Chambers tore around the parking lot and back out onto the main road.

"Shit, Chambers! Where did you learn to drive? Caesars Palace?"

"Shut up." Chambers growled. "Have you managed to get hold of Emily?"

"No, she's beginning to hang up." Mike stared at the six calls he had made to Emily as he paced around the parking lot. "I don't know what's going on now."

"But you're sure that something's amiss."

"Prudence said Callie tried to get hold of me but I have no evidence of it. And Emily and Callie are friendly enough, but I don't recall being friendly enough to call each other except in work emergencies."

"She's being used as bait?"

"I'm beginning to think so."

Chambers shook his head.

"That's just like Emily. She will drop everything to help something."

"I've known that since I met her."

Chambers grunted. Then he gestured towards the back seat.

"I had a call from Major Warden. He had something for you. He emailed it over."

There was a file on the back seat. Mike grabbed it before it slipped onto the floor.

"What is it?"

"Shelley Barton's file. Did you know Emily's ex Houghton-Leathers had a sister?"

"What? No, I didn't. I don't think Emily knew, either."

"There's a good chance she didn't." Chambers swerved his car around a dawdling vehicle, getting a horn hooted loudly at him in response. "Shelley and Darryl were twins, separated by the care system when they were five. They connected a few years ago, and there's evidence that Shelley met Marsden around the same time."

"She pretended to be his lawyer to get unfettered access to Marsden while he was in jail." Mike murmured. "Booty call or planning a break-out?"

"Probably both. We can't assume too much right now." Chambers scowled. "Her enlistment papers are in that file as well."

"She tried to get into the army?"

"Yes. But she was turned down. Her psychology report is in there. Top sheet."

Mike opened the file and scanned the report. It took a moment for the words to sink in.

"Sociopathic tendencies. History of depression and the psychologist suspects bipolar disorder, possibly some other mental health problems. She was a complete mess."

"That's essentially what I summed it up as. Major Warden said he had never seen that much in a psychologist's report before."

"Other soldiers have managed to enlist with more. Why did she get refused?"

"Check the bottom bit."

Mike did. And he went cold.

"Barton confessed to killing a friend when she was ten. The records were sealed because she was underage and she went to juvie. Shit. Why would she tell the psychologist about that? If that were me, I'd keep quiet about the murder."

"Sounds like she thought nobody could touch her as she had gotten away with just a light sentence." Chambers said grimly. "She couldn't get into the army, so Barton got as close as she could get afterwards. Various jobs where she was in close contact with soldiers. Bounced around quite a bit. From what Major Warden managed to get, the girl is obsessed with anything to do with the army."

It sounded like Shelley Barton was more psychotic than Marsden. If she was the partner, she would be a very willing one.

Then Mike saw a picture sticking out from the papers. He drew it out. It was of a black woman with short curly hair looking blankly at the camera. It looked like one of those pictures taken to put on a driver's license.

Mike stared. *Oh, shit. It couldn't be. How was this possible?*

"Wilson?" Chambers glanced at him. "You know her?"

"Oh, yes." Mike felt his stomach drop. "I know her. She works for me."

Chapter Nineteen

Emily stirred with a moan. Her head hurt. Her lip was throbbing, and her cheek was sore. What had hit her? She tried to bring a hand up to her head, but found that she couldn't. Something was holding her wrist to something, and her restraints were digging into her skin.

What was going on?

Then it came back to her. She had gone to help Callie. Someone had threatened her. And then...

She called me Emily. She knew.

"Oh, good, you're awake." A familiar voice came from somewhere in front of her. "I was beginning to think your head was not as hard as I thought."

Emily looked up, blinking into the darkness. She was at one of the corner tables in the restaurant, her placing out of sight of the front windows. She was tied to a chair, her wrists secured to the arms with zip-ties. Another rope was wrapped around her chest, her back plastered against the back of the chair.

Callie was sitting across from her, leaning back in her chair with her feet propped up and crossed on the table. A gun was on the table in front of her.

No. This wasn't Callie. Emily felt clarity sink in.

"Why are you doing this, Shelley?"

Callie raised her eyebrows, no surprise in her expression.

"I was beginning to think you'd never figure it out."

"You didn't exactly make it easy." Emily nodded at Callie's face. " Prudence gave you that black eye, didn't she?"

Callie grimaced.

"She's got a good wallop on her, I'll give her that. I'll go back and sort her out when I've dealt with you."

Emily stiffened. She tugged at her restraints, but they didn't budge. If anything, they seemed to get tighter around her wrists. She winced as they bit in. Callie snorted.

"Come on, Emily, you didn't think I'd make it easy for you to get out? Even if you manage to get out, I've got your weapons." She tittered. "You've proven to be a slippery character. Eddie made the mistake of attacking you when you could fight back. I'm not doing that."

"Why are you doing this, Shelley? What did I ever do to you?"

"You put the man I love behind bars." Callie lowered her legs and sat forward, jabbing her finger into the tabel. "He did nothing wrong."

Emily stared.

"Are you mad? Did you not see his home? Did you see the injuries on Susan Grey?"

Callie snorted.

"Susan was good at lying. She should've kept her mouth shut if she didn't get her own way. And Eddie's never touched me like that. He loves me."

"Give it time and he would have shown the real person he was."

"Not a chance. Eddie and I are soulmates. Susan wasn't good for him. She knew how to push his buttons."

"Oh, really." Emily narrowed her eyes. "Is that why you killed her?"

Callie shrugged with a satisfied smirk.

"Eddie said I could do it. And I took pleasure in it. The pain in her eyes when I finally killed her…" She sighed. "It was exquisite."

Emily felt sick.

"You're disgusting."

"And you think you're not? You arrested him, you and those bozos in the MPs. Darryl and I weren't having it."

"Darryl was in on it as well?"

"Of course he was. Eddie and Darryl did everything together. They were as thick as thieves. Darryl would have done anything for Eddie. We got him out that night and Darryl gave him the key to your house." Callie's lip curled in a sneer. "When you survived and disappeared, we thought we had lost the chance. So, we went after the others."

Hearing confirmation that her ex had been involved made Emily feel like she was going to throw up. She had lain with a man who had harbored a criminal.

"Who killed the people involved? Was it Marsden or you? Did Darryl join in?"

"We had a number to choose from. So we just drew them from a hat." Callie rolled her eyes. "Darryl went after the judge, but that didn't work. The stubborn bugger is still alive."

"He'll never be able to walk again."

"That's something. The lawyers…they were easy pickings. And so much fun." Callie giggled. "Darryl wanted to save you for last, but your team was tougher than we thought to get close to. Eddie didn't want to wait. You were the one who arrested him, and he wanted to deal with you personally."

"By taunting me with dead bodies?"

"That was my idea. Dead body meant you were going to be the same before the day was done." Callie sighed. "And we failed. Twice."

"You managed to get through Mike's alarms and defences at his house." Emily muttered. "I wouldn't say you failed."

"Disabling that was easy. But you were loose and kicking." Callie ran her fingers over the gun on the table. "I told Eddie that you would need to be immobilized before he killed you, but he loved a challenge. And you proved too much of a challenge."

"Glad to know I can do something right." Emily licked her lips. She could only hope that Mike had smelled a rat and was on his way. If not, she was screwed. "How long had you known where I was?"

"Within a month of you disappearing. We knew there had to be a paper trail somewhere. I sneaked into your colonel's office and managed to find the file of where you'd gone. Nobody looks twice at a cleaner." Callie shrugged. "Once we knew where you were, it was easy enough to get a job at this place myself. I knew who you were as soon as I saw you." She gestured at Emily's hair. "You should've died your mop. That might have made it a bit tougher."

164

Emily didn't respond to that. She needed Callie to keep talking. The more she talked, the more she could think of a way to get out. And Emily was coming up short.

"Knowing where you were was the easy thing. But being under Wilson's watchful eye was going to make it tough. Just a couple of weeks here and I could see that he was very protective about you. We had to take our time, which made Eddie antsy."

The zip-ties were digging more into her wrists. Emily glanced down and saw the blood trickling onto the armrest. She gritted her teeth, trying to focus on Callie. Coupled with her throbbing head, it was getting tougher to stay conscious.

"You do know that Eddie's been arrested again. Once he's out of surgery, he's going back to Tacoma."

"I know. I've already seen him. But he won't be in custody for much longer." Callie grinned. "Not when this case falls apart."

Emily stared.

"You think he's going to walk away from this? He's bang to rights."

"I'm good at spinning things. We'll manage."

Emily bit back a snarl. She had worked hard on bringing Marsden before a court and putting him away. She wasn't about to have him walk free, able to come after her again.

"What about Darryl?" She demanded. "What did Darryl do that got him killed?"

Callie snorted.

"He was starting to get a conscience. The pathetic bastard still carries a torch for you. And he said he was going to tell you everything, tell the police what was going on. Cut a deal." Callie shook her head. "We couldn't let that happen. Eddie was busy watching you, so I said I would deal with him."

"You killed your own brother?"

Callie shrugged.

"If it keeps the man I love out of prison, I'll do anything."

"You're insane."

Callie arched an eyebrow.

"You think I'm insane. You haven't seen anything yet." Her fingers toyed on the gun again. "I did want to torture you before I killed you, take some pleasure in seeing the fight go out of you. But I want to wait until Mike clicks that you're in trouble. It shouldn't take long before he gets here. If he's as smart as we think he is, he'll be here soon to watch you die."

She was going to kill her in front of Mike. Emily went cold. The woman sitting in front of her was not the same person who had worked alongside her for seven months. This was a cold-hearted psychopath. She was willing to kill anyone to get the man she loved free.

"You're enjoying this, aren't you?"

Callie smirked.

"Always." She picked up the gun and pointed it at Emily's head. "Now you shut up. I don't want you giving us away just yet."

#

Chambers performed a sharp turn into the parking lot that had Mike clutching onto the car door before he got thrown against it, screeching to a stop outside the fire escape. Then Chambers reached into the glove compartment and brought out a gun and full clip.

"You armed, Wilson?" He asked, loading the clip and feeding a bullet into the chamber.

"Of course." Mike got out of the car, retrieving his gun from the back of his jeans. He took the safety off. "You go high, I go low?"

Chambers snorted.

"I always go high. I'm not out of the running yet."

Mike didn't doubt that. He hurried over to the fire escape, which was open a crack. Chambers crept up behind him as Mike checked the door. Nothing made a noise as he opened it, and nothing went off bang. Taking a deep breath, Mike went inside in a crouch. Chambers followed him, his footsteps as silent as Mike's own. Mike raised a hand and pressed a finger to his lips.

"I hear voices." He whispered. "Out in the main room."

"Do you recognize them?"

Mike listened closely. One was Emily. She sounded in pain, but at least she was alive. And the other was Callie.

Callie. Shelley Barton. How did she manage to keep up a facade for so long? His manager had certainly played a good game on all of them.

"Yes. They're both in there." Mike pointed at the door. "It's me she's expecting. Cover me."

"Yes, Sergeant."

Mike saw the roll of the man's eyes and bit back a smile. It wasn't often he got to tell a colonel what to do. Keeping his gun up, Mike pulled at the door and stepped into the restaurant. It was scarily quiet. All the lights were off, everything stacked up for the night. Mike had never noticed the eerie quality of the place.

Voices were coming from one of the tables behind the booths. Mike headed through the tables, keeping close to the wall. Then he saw them. Emily was tied to one of the chairs, blood trickling from her forehead with a rope around her chest. She was gritting her teeth hard, and Mike saw the flash of pain across her face. Callie sat across from her, a gun pointed at Emily's face. The gun wasn't wavering. If Mike made a sudden move, Emily was getting a bullet between the eyes.

Lowering his gun and keeping his hands up, his finger off the trigger, Mike moved around the plant he had been using for cover. Emily saw him first and her eyes widened. Callie barely glanced over her shoulder, simply rising to her feet and moving so she could see both of them. The gun never wobbled.

"Hey, Mike." Callie leaned against the wall. "I was beginning to wonder if you were going to turn up."

"I had a suspicion when you claimed to have called me and you didn't." Mike glanced at Emily. Then he saw the blood on one of her wrists, smudged around the bindings. "You won't be able to walk out of here, Shelley."

Callie arched an eyebrow.

"You've found out who I am as well, have you? I shouldn't be surprised. You've got your sources."

"Once we knew where to look, it was easy." Mike shifted closer, ever so slowly. "I have backup. You won't be walking out of here."

"Oh, I will. If you want your girl to live, you'll let me walk."

"You know I can't do that."

"You'd happily let Emily die?"

Mike glanced at Emily. She looked up at her and he saw her emotions shut down. She went back to the cold, stern soldier he had seen when Marsden attacked. Putting everything into a box for later. Emily gave him a slight nod. She was ready for a fight.

Hopefully, it wouldn't come to that.

"Oh, how sweet." Callie sneered. "Such a sweet moment. Too bad it won't happen too much longer."

"You're mad if you think you'll be able to walk away from yet another murder, Shelley."

"I did it before. I can do it again."

"Doesn't work like that and you know it."

Callie snorted. Her jaw tightened.

"You two had what I wanted for so many years. I wanted to be a squaddie, too. Have that camaraderie you see. Be part of a unit for the first time in my life, especially when I knew Darryl had enlisted successfully. And they refused to let me in. They said I was too unstable." Callie scowled, pushing off the wall. "What a crock! I have never been unstable. I would have been one of the best they ever had."

"You murdered a child when you were ten." Mike pointed out.

Emily gasped. Callie rolled her eyes.

"Come on, as if that matters. Nothing matters if it happens before you're eighteen. They shouldn't have taken that into account."

"The army takes everything into account, especially if you start gloating about it." Mike shifted closer again. If he was a little closer, he could jump her. He could get the gun away before Emily got hurt. "Give yourself up, Shelley. It won't be easy for you if you fight it."

"I never make things easy." Callie swung the gun around to point at Mike's face. "If you bastards can fit Eddie up, you can fit me up. I won't see the inside of a courtroom."

"Is that a promise?"

Callie smirked. Her eyes seemed to glow almost manically.

"You bet."

She started to turn back to Emily. Mike aimed, but he fired too late. Callie had fired one shot just as Emily threw herself to the side. The bullet hit the panelling where her head had been. Then Callie jerked once as Mike's shot hit her in the chest, and again as another shot rang out. Callie hit the wall, a stunned look in her eyes. She remained frozen for a moment, and then slid down the wall. Blood coated the wall behind her and she slumped on the floor.

Mike's ears were ringing. His head was pounding. Then he was snapped out of his daze by Chambers. The colonel stepped around him and headed to where Callie lay, still with her eyes open.

"I'll deal with her." Chambers knelt, checking for Callie's pulse. "You deal with Emily. Sergeant!"

The final bark had Mike moving again. Emily lay on the floor, still tied to the chair and unmoving. Mike fell to his knees and dug into his back pocket for his knife. His hands shook as he sliced through the zip-ties, managing to undo the knot in the rope. Emily moaned as the bindings came loose, slumping to the floor and curling into a ball. Mike gently lifted her up, cradling her on his lap as he checked her over. Her head was bleeding, and her wrists were red raw and cut up. Tucking her against his chest, Mike stroked her hair.

"Emily. Emily, talk to me. Let me know you're okay."

"What? Mike?" Emily sounded dazed. Her expression was dazed as she looked up at him. "What happened?"

"You just took another knock to the head." Mike kissed her head. "Give yourself a moment."

Behind him, he heard Chambers calling for an ambulance. Callie must still be alive. Mike focused on the woman in his arms, rocking her gently as Emily came back to her senses.

"Where's Callie?" Emily licked her lips, her voice sounding dry. "Did you get her?"

Mike glanced over his shoulder. Callie was still leaning against the wall, and she was still breathing. Chambers was pressing on the wounds trying to stop the bleeding.

"Yeah. We got her."

From the look of it, Callie wasn't going anywhere.

Chapter Twenty

The paramedics said she would need to go to hospital to check for a concussion. Emily hated hospitals. She could do without. The paramedic who looked her over in Mike's office didn't look too happy about Emily refusing further medical treatment, muttering under his breath about 'damn squaddies'. Emily didn't care as long as she didn't have to go to hospital.

At least she was in better condition than Callie. Callie had taken two bullets to the chest. Non-fatal, from what Chambers said, but it was enough to make her condition critical. Chambers was going to ride with her and keep watch until the cops arrived to take over guard duty. Then she would be charged with murder and various other charges once she recovered.

And she would. Chambers had been confident that his shot was non-fatal. So was Mike. Emily had no idea as she was busy throwing herself out of the way of a bullet. Her body was still aching from being tied to that damn chair.

The paramedic left her alone, Emily huddling in a blanket Mike had draped around her shoulders. Her head felt like it was about to explode. Maybe she should have taken them up on the offer to go and get a head scan, but Emily didn't want to be anywhere near a hospital. She wanted to go home.

Home. What conjured up in her mind when she thought of home was not Tacoma. It was Mike's home. In just two days, his home had become hers.

Leaving Union to go back to Tacoma would be next to impossible now after that revelation. Emily just hoped she wasn't going to have a broken heart when she laid everything bare to Mike.

From the way things have been going, you shouldn't have anything to worry

171

about.

Shouldn't I?

Emily looked up as the door opened. Mike entered, his shoulders slumped in exhaustion. Then he looked up at Emily, and he smiled, which softened the harsh lines on his face. Emily found herself smiling back.

"Hey. Have the masses left yet?"

"The cops are still working on the scene downstairs. Winston wants to talk to you in a bit."

Emily sighed heavily and rubbed her eyes.

"As long as he doesn't take too long. I want to go home."

There was silence. Emily looked up. Mike was watching her with a guarded look. He swallowed.

"And where would home be for you, Emily?" He whispered.

Emily smiled and rose to her feet.

"I'd like to say it was with you. If you'll have me, that is."

Mike stared at her. Then he strode across the room and kissed her, cupping her head with a gentle touch. Emily could feel her head complaining about even that, but she didn't care. Mike rested his forehead against hers.

"I'll always have you, Emily. And you're welcome to my home." He kissed her and stroked her cheek, sliding his fingers down her neck to her shoulder. "If you were going back to Tacoma, I was going to say that I was coming with you."

"What?" Emily drew back. "You would have given everything up to follow me?"

"I can sell this place and start a new one. And Prudence is going to college as soon as her summer classes have completed. I won't have anyone tying me down to one place." Mike hesitated. "Except you. Does that sound a little too much?"

"Coming from anyone else, yes." Emily stared at him. "That doesn't sound like you at all, Mike. I didn't think you would drop everything for one person."

Mike's cheeks flushed.

"I didn't think I would, either. But you're proving me wrong." He wrapped his arms around her, kissing her softly. "I love you, Emily. And I don't want to let you walk away from me now."

He loved her. Emily felt really warm hearing that. She smiled and snuggled into him, kissing his jaw.

"I'm happy to stay here in Union, as long as you're here. It just so happens," she added as she tugged his head down, "that I love you, too. I would happily commit to moving here permanently."

"Really?" Mike began to smile as she kissed him. "You would really stay here?"

"Definitely." Emily made a face. "As long as I don't work as a waitress. That job is hell."

Mike threw back his head and laughed.

"Yeah, and I would be seriously distracted watching you with the customers. But I've got a better idea." He brushed her hair away from her face, twirling a curl around his finger. "How about becoming an equal partner in this business?"

"Really?" Emily stared. "Do you mean it?"

"Yes. I wouldn't share this place with just anyone. They would have to be special. I would work downstairs with the customers and you can do the admin."

Emily groaned.

"It would be me doing the admin, wouldn't it?"

"Well, you're better than I am." Mike chuckled. "You wouldn't need to walk around talking to college jocks who think they can paw you like you're on the menu."

"Mostly because you would rip them to pieces."

"After what I've just confessed to, absolutely."

Emily giggled.

"I'd like to see that, though." She wrapped her arms around his neck. "And what sort of perks would I get for doing the admin side of the business? What incentive do I have?"

"How about unfettered access to me?" Mike palmed her backside, kissing along her jaw to her ear. "You get to do what you want to me. I'm open to suggestions."

"I thought you liked control in the bedroom."

"Even those who like control can hand it over for a while." Mike sighed as he nuzzled her neck. "And I'd happily hand it to you. If you can manage an old man."

"Hey!" Emily slapped his shoulder. "You're not old. How many times do I have to say it?"

"My stamina isn't not going to be there forever."

"Neither is mine." Emily nipped at his bottom teeth with her lip. "I'm sure we can...figure something out. But you'll have to commit to your promise to let me take charge in bed."

Mike grinned, taking her mouth in a deep kiss.

"Oh, I'm going to commit." He promised. "I'm going to be doing a lot of that."

Also in This Series

Agent Silver

Lisa had no idea what her mother was up to. Not until she was murdered. And now those Special Agent Katie Higgins was investigating are coming after Lisa. The one she turns to is the one man she can trust. And one she can't have.

Giles is a family friend and a colleague of Katie's. He sees it as a duty to protect Lisa. But he's not supposed to want her like a man wants a woman. He made a promise, and he's not going to break it. Even if it means going through his own personal hell...

Deputy Silver

Laura is a rookie FBI agent, and she's going up the ranks fast. When she's given the chance to work with local law enforcement over a sudden series of murders that seem to be linked, Laura jumps at the chance so she can go into the department she wants to be in. The fact that she has to tussle with the older deputy sheriff who's been assigned to her doesn't faze her. Much...

Cameron is one of the most experienced deputies in his department. He knows how to run an investigation, and he doesn't want an FBI agent treading on his toes. Certainly not one younger than his daughter. If she wasn't so beautiful and smart, she wouldn't be such a distraction...

Also By the Author

A Day To Remember
   Snowed In: Michael and Spyros
   An Education
   Unable to Move On
   Resurfaced
   Walrider's Woman
   Below Stairs
   Married to the Invader
   Trapped With the Boss
   Major Lockdown
   Distanced No More

Coming Soon:
Candy Shop Series 13: His Red-Blooded Heart Throb (release date 13th June)

About the Author

Katharine has loved writing since she was young. At the start she wrote crime, and then switched over to romance when her work gravitated in that direction. She graduated from the University of Derby in 2010 in Creative Writing and Film and TV Studies, and wrote as a hobby while she worked as a community care worker. In 2014, she left care work and became a full-time mother, turning to fully focus on her writing. Since October 2015, Katharine has been a freelance ghostwriter, focusing mainly on romantic fiction in a variety of genres. In June 2018, she published her first book A Day to Remember.

Katharine lives in Derby with her fiancé and her two young children. When she isn't writing, she's playing field hockey on the weekends or acting as a taxi for her children and their multiple activities. She loves to read and likes watching a lot of consumer programs.

For more information, please visit facebook.com/katharine.budd.

Printed in Poland
by Amazon Fulfillment
Poland Sp. z o.o., Wrocław

59403322R00108